"Everyone

Shane looked

impression tha the

dog anymore. D identify with homeless, unloved creatures? He found himself more than a little curious about this pushy, headstrong officer.

Looking at her, he wouldn't have thought she was unloved at all. Quite the opposite. But then, he'd come to recognize that self-image had little to do with what a person saw reflected in their mirror in the morning.

"After you lost your parents, did any of your relatives step up?" He saw a dark look enter Ashley's eyes, a look that warned him to back off now if he knew what was good for him. But he was already in this.

Her voice was a little strained when she finally did answer his question.

Strained and distant.

"They couldn't determine who my parents were. The interior of the car had burned to a crisp, as had the two people in it. No identification of any kind was ever found."

Cavanaugh Justice: Where the law and passion collide....

Dear Reader,

Welcome back to the Cavanaughs. I am always being asked where I get my ideas from. My answer is always the same. Everywhere. The idea for this story initially came from a morning talk show. It featured a story about perfectly sane, ordinary women who had ordinary careers—and went through their days pushing strollers, changing diapers, carrying bundles of joy in their arms. The only difference between them and other mothers who were doing the same thing was that their babies were created in a factory. They felt real, smelled real, some had a "heartbeat," others turned if you touched them a certain way. But, like Peter Pan, these babies never grow up. You take that extreme behavior, push it a little further, you could very well have a situation like the one I write about here.

I'm very lucky in my profession. The stories are everywhere. I hope you like this one and that you enjoy your stay with the Cavanaughs enough to come back again next time. I promise you won't be bored.

As ever, I thank you for reading and from the bottom of my heart, I wish you someone to love who loves you back.

All my best,

Marie

MISSION: CAVANAUGH BABY

Marie Ferrarella

HARLEQUIN® ROMANTIC SUSPENSE

Recycling programs for this product may not exist in your area.

ISBN-13: 978-0-373-27837-4

MISSION: CAVANAUGH BABY

This edition published by arrangement with Harlequin Books S.A.

For questions and comments about the quality of this book, please contact us at CustomerService@Harlequin.com.

Printed in U.S.A.

Books by Marie Ferrarella

Harlequin Romantic Suspense

Private Justice #1664
***The Doctor's Guardian #1675*
**A Cavanaugh Christmas #1683*
Special Agent's Perfect Cover #1688
**Cavanaugh's Bodyguard #1699*
**Cavanaugh Rules #1715*
**Cavanaugh's Surrender #1725*
Colton Showdown #1732
A Widow's Guilty Secret #1736
**Cavanaugh on Duty #1751*
†The Colton Ransom #1760
**Mission: Cavanaugh Baby #1767*

Harlequin Special Edition

†††A Match for the Doctor #2117
†††What the Single Dad Wants... #2122
^The Baby Wore a Badge #2131
#Fortune's Valentine Bride #2167
†††Once Upon a Matchmaker #2192
-Real Vintage Maverick #2210
†††A Perfectly Imperfect Match #2240
****A Small Fortune #2246*
†††Ten Years Later... #2252
†††Wish Upon a Matchmaker #2264

Silhouette Special Edition

‡Diamond in the Rough #1910
‡The Bride with No Name #1917
‡Mistletoe and Miracles #1941
†Plain Jane and the Playboy #1946
‡Travis's Appeal #1958
Loving the Right Brother #1977
The 39-Year-Old Virgin #1983
‡A Lawman for Christmas #2006
††Prescription for Romance #2017
†††Doctoring the Single Dad #2031
†††Fixed Up with Mr. Right? #2041
†††Finding Happily-Ever-After #2060
†††Unwrapping the Playboy #2084
‡‡Fortune's Just Desserts #2107

Silhouette Romantic Suspense

***A Doctor's Secret #1503*
***Secret Agent Affair #1511*
**Protecting His Witness #1515*
Colton's Secret Service #1528
The Heiress's 2-Week Affair #1556
**Cavanaugh Pride #1571*
**Becoming a Cavanaugh #1575*
The Agent's Secret Baby #1580
**The Cavanaugh Code #1587*
**In Bed with the Badge #1596*
**Cavanaugh Judgment #1612*
Colton by Marriage #1616
**Cavanaugh Reunion #1623*
***In His Protective Custody #1644*

Harlequin American Romance

Pocketful of Rainbows #145
‡‡‡The Sheriff's Christmas Surprise #1329
†††Ramona and the Renegade #1338
‡‡‡The Doctor's Forever Family #1346
Montana Sheriff #1369
Holiday in a Stetson #1378
"The Sheriff Who Found Christmas"
‡‡‡Lassoing the Deputy #1402
‡‡‡A Baby on the Ranch #1410
‡‡‡A Forever Christmas #1426
‡‡‡His Forever Valentine #1462

*Cavanaugh Justice
***The Doctors Pulaski*
‡Kate's Boys
†The Fortunes of Texas: Return to Red Rock
††The Baby Chase
†††Matchmaking Mamas
‡‡The Fortunes of Texas: Lost...and Found
‡‡‡Forever, Texas
^Montana Mavericks:
The Texans Are Coming!
#The Fortunes of Texas: Whirlwind Romance
-Montana Mavericks: Back in the Saddle
***The Fortunes of Texas: Southern Invasion
†The Coltons of Wyoming

Other titles by this author available in ebook format.

MARIE FERRARELLA

This *USA TODAY* bestselling and RITA® Award-winning author has written more than two hundred books for Harlequin, some under the name Marie Nicole. Her romances are beloved by fans worldwide. Visit her website, www.marieferrarella.com.

To
Jessi & Nik,
the two best things
I ever produced.

Prologue

She didn't want to wake her babies.

Stepping into the bedroom she had turned into a beautiful, fairy-tale-like nursery, the short, maternal-looking woman eased the door closed behind her, careful not to make a sound.

Her deep-set brown eyes swept over all three of the delicate, snow-white, Angelina Six Leg cribs in the room, each placed against a different wall so that she had room to move around, room to scoop up whichever infant needed her at the moment. The cribs, with their hand-carved headboards were identical and very expensive, but nothing was too good for her babies.

Tiptoeing over to the first crib, she looked down

at Adele and smiled. Her eyes were closed. She was still asleep.

Unable to resist, Tessie placed her hand ever so lightly on the small tummy, barely making contact. Even so, she could feel Adele breathing. The simple up and down movement filled her with a sense of awe as well as joy. Adele had been her first.

"You go on sleeping, sweetheart," Tessie whispered softly, "so you can grow up big and strong. Mama loves you."

The heavyset woman then made her way to the next crib.

Maureen appeared to be fast asleep, as well. Even so, when Tessie gently brushed her fingertips along the infant's smooth, silky cheek, she saw the tiny rosebud mouth begin to root around, as if she was searching for her bottle.

This one was going to wake up hungry, Tessie thought, lingering over the crib.

"I'd better get your bottle ready, little one," she murmured softly.

As Tessie drew her hand back, she accidentally brushed it against Maureen's tightly closed fist. Even in sleep, the infant reacted. Her fingers closed around Tessie's finger, creating a link—a brand-new life connecting to one that had been around for more than five decades.

Tessie stood over the crib for several moments, absorbing the warm sensations she always felt whenever Maureen would grasp her finger this way.

The helplessness of the infant before her branded her heart. Maureen was completely dependent on her for everything, as were Adele and the occupant of the third crib, Cathy.

The sense of responsibility she was feeling humbled Tessie, the way it always did.

Disengaging her finger from Maureen's grasp, Tessie made her way over to the third crib a little more slowly. There was rain in the air, and that always seemed to bother her arthritic knees.

Cathy was her favorite, although she would never allow the other two to suspect this. She knew she wasn't supposed to have favorites, but she couldn't help herself. Whenever she approached and touched Cathy, the infant would turn her head to look at her, as if Cathy had recognized her from the very first.

It felt as if they had bonded the second Cathy had come into her life.

Tessie had thought perhaps this was all just a happy coincidence, Cathy turning her head and making eye contact when she touched the baby, but it wasn't. Cathy actually responded to her, would look to find her no matter which side of the crib she stood on. Those electric-blue eyes would always seek her out.

"Well hello, Night Owl," Tessie cooed over the infant. "I see you're still awake." Tessie chuckled. "Somehow, I knew you would be. Tell you what, what do you say to letting your sisters stay in dreamland while just the two of us go off? You and I have a date with a warm bottle and a rocking chair." Tessie smiled at the small figure in the large crib. "There might even be a lullaby in it for you if you don't make a sound to wake your sisters."

Bending over the crib, the woman placed her hands carefully beneath the precious bundle and silently lifted her into her arms. Cathy turned her head as if to watch her and make sure that everything was all right.

Placing the baby against her shoulder, Tessie could feel the infant's weight shifting, could feel her tiny body melding against her.

She never grew tired of that sensation. It filled her with love and the desire to protect these tiny little beings with the last ounce of breath in her body.

She patted Cathy's back as she withdrew from the room. Cathy didn't make a sound.

"Good girl," Tessie whispered. "You didn't wake your sisters."

Leaving the room as softly as she had entered, Tessie closed the door again so that no outside noises could rouse either Adele or Maureen. After all, she only had two hands, and one baby at a time was really all she could handle.

Despite the fact that the door to the nursery was closed, Tessie still kept her voice to a whisper. "I don't know where your bottle got to, so I'm using Maureen's. I won't tell if you don't," she said to the infant, chuckling.

Cathy remained silent.

Tessie's smile spread. "I'll take that as a yes," she said, pleased. "When the new little one comes," she continued as she walked through the house to get to the kitchen, "I'm going to be counting on you to show her the ropes."

Not making a sound, Cathy continued to look at her, appearing to hang on every word that was said.

Chapter 1

"Get that needy little face away from me. I'm onto you, Rusty." Glancing at the worn-out analog watch that was never off her wrist except when she was showering, Officer Ashley St. James shook her head as she moved about her small bedroom, trying to get ready for work. "I've got just enough time to put your breakfast out, so stop dancing around trying to trip me or I'm going to be late—and I can't afford to be late again this month. The lieutenant is *not* a forgiving man, understand?"

Two sets of eyes looked up at her, and it seemed for all the world as if the creatures behind those eyes were hanging on her every word.

Ashley knew better.

Rusty and his cohort in crime only heard what

they *wanted* to hear. Right now, what they both appeared to want to hear was simply the sound of her voice. They didn't want her to leave. They wanted her to stay and play with them.

She only wished she could oblige.

"Out of my way, boys," Ashley ordered, sweeping past the furry duo and making her way to the kitchen. Her entourage followed swiftly in her wake. Anticipation, Ashley could tell, was in the air.

Her routine was second nature to her. Quickly distributing equal amounts of food between two bowls, Ashley carried them over to the corner of the kitchen where the two dogs she'd rescued always ate.

Ordinarily that would be enough for Olympic-speed chewing to begin. But this morning, the two canines she shared her home with seemed far more interested in surrounding her—thereby outnumbering her—and loudly protesting the fact that she was just about to leave the house.

When they barked like that, they sounded more like a pack of dogs than just two.

Ashley put her hands on her hips and gave each culprit a look that was meant to silence them. "C'mon, guys, no more fooling around—or there'll be *no treats* when I get home."

That, she noted with no small satisfaction, combined with her I'm-not-kidding look, seemed to do the trick. The two dogs immediately stopped barking and turned their attention to the bowls brimming with food as a consolation prize.

"It's not that I don't appreciate the love and affection, I do," she told them, rushing around the kitchen, attempting to restore it to reasonable order before she left.

If there was anything she couldn't stand, it was a messy kitchen. Coming home to one after her shift was over was downright disheartening to her. And she would only have herself to blame if it was in a total state of chaos. Initially the dogs, both of which she'd rescued once it was clear that each had been abandoned by their former owners, had no problem showing their displeasure if she did something they weren't happy about. They soon learned that pulling open the bottom drawer of her bureau and dragging it clear across the first floor, then emptying its contents and making a home in her underwear, was *not* acceptable.

Still, she could tell that they really wanted her to stay. That was what she got for spending the weekend catering to them and playing with them. They took to that instantly and seemed to think it was going to be like that from then on.

She only wished they were right. But life wasn't that simple.

"I know, I know, if it was up to you, we'd all hang out together and I'd never leave the house. But if that happened, how would I earn the money to feed you two gluttonous creatures, never mind getting it to the house? The pet store doesn't make deliveries."

In response to her question, the dogs just continued eating as if the food before them was about to vanish at any second.

"I swear," Ashley murmured, glancing at the empty bowls, "if I hadn't just had you two checked out by the police department's vet, I would bet anything that you're both at the mercy of a couple of tapeworms." She paused to pet the dog closest to her, a golden Labrador that looked as if he'd been deliberately shrunk in the wash. He certainly didn't look overweight. "Where do you *put* it, Rusty?" she mused.

Not to be left out, Dakota, a five-year-old German shepherd, ducked under her hand and pushed it with his head, moving it away from the Labrador. He took the lion's share of her hand for himself.

Ashley laughed. "Certainly make your wishes well known, don't you, boy?" she asked.

In response, the German shepherd continued nuzzling her. Not to be outdone, the Labrador circled around to her other side. He was definitely lobbying for a space beside her.

Time to go, she thought, rising to her feet.

"Okay, guys, I'm serious now. You heard me. Back up." The German shepherd responded to her sharp tone while the Labrador, as if convinced that she was only being blustery for form's sake, not only didn't back up out of her way, but licked her fingertips.

"Sorry, not going to work this time, Dakota. If I'm *ever* going to work my way out of the Animal

Control Division and into some kind of investigative department, I can't show up late. Can you just hear the excuse if they ask me why I didn't come in when I was supposed to?

"'Why are you late, Officer St. James?' 'Because my dogs wouldn't let me leave my house.'" She pressed her lips together, attempting to look as if she was frowning—as if she could *ever* be mad at her pets. "Not exactly something someone working in Animal Control should really admit to, is it?" she asked her dogs.

The German shepherd barked as if he agreed with her. At least, that was the way she wanted to interpret his bark. For once, Rusty abstained from the debate.

Ashley grinned. "I know why you're doing it, you know. You're trying to keep me home because you're just afraid I'm going to bring home another stray." She ran a hand over each of the dogs. They constituted her only family, as well as her best friends. "Even if I did, that doesn't mean I'd stop caring about you two. You're my whole world. Now take those cute little butts and get them out of my way," Ashley instructed.

One more glance at her watch told her that she was *really* going to have to hustle to get to the police station on time.

"See you guys tonight," she called over her shoulder as she went out the front door. "And don't give the mail carrier a heart attack if he comes up to the front door to leave a package," she warned. "The poor guy's just doing his job."

Leaving, Ashley paused to lock the front door. Not that she really had to. For its size, Aurora was deemed to be one of the safer cities in the country, but even if it wasn't, she was confident that the sound of Dakota barking up a storm would be more than enough to convince any would-be burglar that it would be a lot smarter to break into another house instead of this one.

Still, it was a habit she'd developed years ago, making sure that whatever was hers—though at the time her possessions had been less than meager—remained hers.

Back then, the only thing she'd had of any worth, really, was the watch she still wore. The old Timex was the only link she had to her past—the only thing she had to prove she even *had* a past. The woman who'd run the home that she'd continuously been sent back to from the time she was four had told her that they'd *thought* the watch belonged to her father, but that they weren't certain. The only thing they'd known was that when they'd found her, she was playing with it.

She'd been discovered sitting on the ground, near the charred remains of a vehicle that had gone off the road, killing the other two occupants of the car, presumably before the car burst into flames. The only reason she had survived was that she'd been thrown clear of the vehicle, sustaining a head injury that had knocked her out for the worst of the fire.

Another couple had called the police to report the accident. The responding officers had taken her to social services. She actually thought she had a vague recollection of a tall officer picking her up and carrying her to the squad car. She recalled the scent of something that smelled like mint.

Since she'd obviously survived the fire untouched, someone at social services had thought it might be clever to call her Ashley—Ash for short. She had no real surname because no ID of any kind had been found on either of the two victims in the car, both of whom had been burned beyond recognition. Consequently, social services had whimsically bestowed a surname on her. She'd been discovered on the last day of March, so she'd become Ashley March.

The moment she'd turned eighteen—or what someone at social services believed *might* be her eighteenth birthday—she'd left the system, and her surname, behind. Having grown accustomed to her first name, she'd christened herself Ashley St. James, James from the name engraved on the back of the oversize watch she was never without.

Squaring her shoulders, Ashley hurried to her used car, ready to face her day.

There were days when she did nothing but drive up and down the peaceful streets of Aurora, searching for strays, birds that had fallen out of nests and couldn't fly and the occasional unlucky animal that had discovered it didn't pay to cross the road when a car was coming.

This morning, however, right after she'd consumed her first cup of tea, her superior, Lieutenant Rener, summoned her into his office.

Wondering if she was about to be given a lecture on the virtues of arriving on time—she had made it by the skin of her teeth, but it was close and the lieutenant was a stickler for discipline—Ashley crossed the threshold with a warm, friendly smile on her face. She'd learned a long time ago to mask every thought, every feeling she had with a smile.

"Officer St. James reporting, sir," she announced the moment she stepped into the lieutenant's rather small office.

Lieutenant Rener barely looked in her direction, acknowledging her presence with a curt nod. He held out an address for her. When she took it, he told her, "Someone called in a disturbance."

That seemed like it should be more under the jurisdiction of the police department that dealt with people, not animals. But for the time being, Ashley held her peace, confident that if an explanation for rerouting this to animal services was in the offing, she would hear it soon enough.

"A woman called to complain about a barking dog," Rener told her.

She glanced at the address. It was for an apartment complex nearby. They were garden apartments, if she recalled correctly. Garden or not, it was sti[illegible] people living on top of each other, she thought, su[illegible] pressing a shiver. She'd had all she could stand [illegible] close quarters during her foster family days—whi[illegible] was why every penny she'd earned had gone towa[illegible] buying a house. She'd lived on ketchup soup a[illegible] mustard sandwiches until she could finally affo[illegible] to put down a down payment on a place of her ow[illegible] Her house was tiny—a forty-five-year-old hou[illegible] with three small bedrooms and a postage-stamp-si[illegible] backyard. It was clear that the place needed wor[illegible] But it was all hers.

"How long has it been barking?" she asked h[illegible] supervisor.

"According to the woman who called in with th[illegible] complaint, all morning." He looked up from the re[illegible] port he was going over. "Go see what you can fi[illegible] out. If the owner's there and the dog's been abus[illegible] or looks like he's been badly neglected, put the fe[illegible] of God into them. Tell the owner if you have to co[illegible] out again, the dog comes back with you," he told h[illegible] as if she was a rookie and didn't know the drill [illegible] heart. "Can't have the good citizens of Aurora li[illegible] tening to nonstop barking."

Ashley couldn't tell if the lieutenant was bei[illegible] sarcastic, droll or was actually on the level with h[illegible] comment.

"Yes, sir," she said, beginning to ease out of th[illegible] office. "Anything else?"

She said it for form's sake. She really didn't expe[illegible] the man to say anything more. But he did and it was equally as unnecessary as what he'd just told her.

"Yeah. If the owner's not around, have the complex manager unlock the apartment for you and bring the animal in with you."

Ashley resisted the very real temptation to roll her eyes at the instruction, which she found to be rather insulting. At the very least, it told her that the lieutenant was *not* paying any attention to her as an employee. She was good at her job, needed next to no instructions and animals seemed to respond to her because she got along better with them than she did the people she had to work with.

People had secrets, they had petty jealousies, they had agendas. With animals, what she saw was what she got. She liked that a lot better.

"Yes, sir," she murmured as she left Rener's office and closed the door behind her.

Ashley could hear the barking even before she parked the small Animal Control van near the apartment and got out.

Rather than aggression, what she heard in the barking was more along the lines of pathetic whining. It was as if the animal was calling to get someone's attention.

Ashley's jaw tightened as anger swept through her. More than likely, the animal had been abused. It was probably chained, starved and beaten, as well. There was nothing she hated more than an animal being the scapegoat for its owner's inadequacies and frustrations. Not to mention that in some cases, abusing and torturing small animals was also the starting point for a budding serial killer.

The dog's pathetic barking felt as if it was reverberating in her chest.

A slender redhead of medium height, Ashley lengthened her stride as she quickened her pace, cutting across the parking lot.

The barking sounded increasingly more pathetic the closer she came to the apartment. She could feel her heart twisting in her chest. That poor dog, she couldn't help thinking. *It sounded as if it was in real pain.*

The apartment the sound was coming from was located on the ground floor. Its kitchen window was facing the parking lot. Rather than knock on the door, Ashley decided to look through the window first to see what she might be up against. Though she loved all breeds of dogs, she wasn't naive about the way some responded to strangers, no matter how well-meaning that stranger might be.

There were blinds at the window, but they were slightly cracked open, just enough for her to be able to see into the apartment.

It took her a few seconds to get her eyes accustomed to the interior of the apartment. A lot of light was *not* coming in, and consequently, a large portion of what she was trying to make out was shrouded in shadow.

Taking out her flashlight, she aimed it at the interior of the apartment.

She saw the dog first. It was a Jack Russell terrier, a breed of dog known to be high-strung and hyper. Clearly agitated, the small, wiry dog was running back and forth around something.

No, some*one*.

Oh, God.

Ashley's mouth dropped open. She could see someone lying on the floor. The flashlight wasn't enough to make out all that much. But there was definitely a person on the kitchen floor.

It was either a woman or a long-haired man. He or she was facedown on the vinyl in what looked like—

Blood.

Dear God, it was blood. Ashley's stomach twisted. Her hand shook as she took out her cell.

Breathe, damn it. Breathe. You've seen blood before, Ash.

She heard a voice on the other end of the line. She wasn't even sure what the voice said. She just launched into her request.

"Dispatch, this is Officer Ashley St. James." She rattled off her badge number as proof of who she was, then said, "I need a bus sent to 198 San Juan. Apartments off Newport Avenue North. Not for an animal, it's for a person," she insisted. "And send backup! Fast!"

Obviously, Dispatch had pulled her badge up on

the computer and would think she was asking for assistance with someone's pet.

Agitated, Ashley barely heard the voice on the other end confirm her request. Terminating the call, she was vaguely aware of pocketing her cell phone. During the call, her eyes never left the figure on the floor.

The dog continued to circle around it, barking and growing progressively more and more agitated, as if it knew that its master couldn't survive long, not with the kind of blood loss that the pool on the floor indicated.

Whoever it was, was bleeding out, Ashley thought. She had to do something. She couldn't just stand there, waiting for the ambulance to arrive.

Her heart in her throat, Ashley raced back to the leasing office to get the manager.

The sign hanging on the closed glass door stopped her in her tracks. "Out showing apartments. Be back in twenty minutes."

The person in the apartment didn't have twenty minutes. He or she might not even have five.

She *had* to get in there, Ashley thought, desperately casting about for how. And then she remembered one of the kids she'd met growing up in the system. He'd taught her a few things that she would never be able to put on a résumé.

Making up her mind, Ashley ran back to the apartment. Scrutinizing the perimeter of the window, she went into action and popped out the left pane, lifting it up and out of the frame. The space was small, but just big enough to accommodate her.

Pulling herself up off the ground, Ashley went through the opening and tumbled into the apartment—into the kitchen sink, more precisely. She hit her shoulder against the metal faucet.

The unexpected jolt vibrated right through her. Entirely focused on the person a few feet away, the pain shooting down her arm barely registered.

The terrier ran toward her, barking furiously, as if to warn her away from the person he was guarding.

For a moment Ashley was certain that the frantic little dog was going to bite her.

"It's okay, boy, it's okay," she told the dog in a low, soothing voice. "I'm here to help. Let me get to your master."

In response, the dog ran back to the person on the floor, as if showing her the way.

"That's it, boy, take me to—"

Ashley's voice felt suddenly trapped in her throat as she quickly followed the terrier to where the person lay.

Horror filled her.

She didn't remember crossing from where she was to the body, but she obviously had to have moved because the next thing Ashley knew she was dropping to her knees beside the victim, panic and a sense of urgency filling her at the same time.

The person on the floor was a woman.

Ashley knew all the rules about touching a victim and disturbing a crime scene. Each one of them began with the word *Don't*.

But she was positive that she could make out just the faintest signs of breathing. The victim's back was moving ever so slightly.

Amid all that blood, there was no visible wound in the back. It clearly had to be in the front.

If this woman had so much as a prayer of making it, Ashley knew that she had to find some way to stop the bleeding.

She began to talk to the victim as if the woman was conscious and could hear her. She talked to her the way she talked to a frightened, wounded animal. Slowly, soothingly.

"I'm with the police department," Ashley said as she turned the woman to face her. "The ambulance is coming. Just hang in there—"

The rest of her words evaporated as she realized that the woman's belly had been slashed open.

Everything began to grow dark, and Ashley struggled not to pass out.

Chapter 2

Exercising every last ounce of her self-control, Ashley fought against the darkness that was trying to swallow her up.

She knew that if she surrendered and passed out, she'd be of no use to the victim. Although it seemed almost improbable, she was positive she'd detected just the slightest movement of the woman's chest. She was struggling to breathe, which meant that the woman was still alive, tethered to life by just the thinnest possible thread.

But any second now, that thread was going to break.

The slash across the woman's abdomen was huge. Ashley stared at it and at the blood, vacillating between nausea and being utterly numb.

There was no way she could possibly manage to stem the flow of the victim's blood using just her hands. She needed something to hold against the gaping wound before the blood completely drained out of the woman.

Quickly stripping off her jacket, Ashley threw it over the wound and pressed down as hard as she could, trying to cover as much of the savage wound as she was able.

In a matter of seconds her jacket turned from light blue to bright red. The blood just continued to ooze out.

"Hang in there," Ashley repeated to the woman, raising her voice so that the victim could hear her. The terrier was still barking frantically. "They're coming. The ambulance is coming. They'll be here any second. Just don't let go."

God, but she wished the paramedics were here already. They were trained, and they'd know what to do to stabilize this woman's vital signs and get her to stop bleeding like this.

She refused to believe that the situation was hopeless. Despite everything that she had been through in her short twenty-five years, there was still a tiny part of Ashley that harbored optimism.

Ashley's heart jumped. The woman's eyelids fluttered, as if she was fighting to stay conscious, but her eyes remained closed. And then Ashley saw the woman's lips moving.

What was she trying to tell her?

"What? I'm sorry, but I can't hear what you're saying." Leaning in as close as she was able, Ashley had her ear all but against the woman's lips. She remained like that as she urged the victim on. "Say it again. Please, your dog's barking too loud for me to hear you."

She thought she heard the woman say something that sounded like "...stole...my...baby."

Ashley couldn't make out the first word for sure, and part of her thought that maybe she'd just imagined the rest of the sentence, but she was positive that she'd felt the woman's warm breath along her face as she tried to tell her something.

And then it hit her. What had happened to this woman wasn't just some random, brutal attack by a deranged psychopath who had broken into her apartment. This was done deliberately.

Someone had kidnapped this woman's baby before it was even born.

Detective Shane Cavanaugh frowned at the piece of paper his captain had just handed him. On it was not only an address, but a confusing short summary of the call that had come in to Dispatch.

It didn't make any sense.

"Am I reading this correctly, Captain?" Sitting at his desk, trying to come to terms with the pile of papers on his desk, Shane read what was written and looked up at the brawny, bald man who had recently been put in charge of the Major Crimes Division.

"I dunno, Cavelli— Sorry, Cavanaugh." The captain corrected himself with a mocking grin. "What is it that you're reading?"

"This call came in from someone with Animal Control asking for backup?" It was half a statement, half a question, but virtually *all* of him didn't care for the captain's attitude toward him.

Captain Owens's tone was condescending. "That's what it says."

"What are we doing taking calls from Animal Control?" Shane wanted to know. "Is business around here that slow lately?"

It hadn't exactly been jumping with cases, but there had been some criminal activity, enough to keep him busy at least since he'd found himself partner-less these past four weeks.

"Apparently, it initially came in as a 'disturbing the peace' call." Owens shrugged his shoulders. "Maybe it escalated. The caller asked for a bus and backup," he said, repeating what he'd written down.

"Just check it out," the captain instructed, then added, "Unless, of course, you feel you're too good for that now, given your new name and all."

Paper in hand, Shane rose from his desk, giving no indication that the captain's verbal jab irritated the hell out of him.

It had been difficult enough accepting the fact that his father, his siblings and he were not actually related to the family he had grown up believing was his, all because of an initial mix-up at the hospital where his father had been born. Suddenly they weren't Italian, they were Scottish.

And now he found himself having to put up with snide remarks rooted in jealousy because when everything was finally cleared up, it came to light that the lot of them was not Cavellis, as they had thought, but Cavanaughs. Which meant, in turn, that he and the others were directly related to Aurora's former chief of police and to the division's current chief of detectives.

In addition, there was a large number of his "new" family who were attached in one capacity or another to the Aurora Police Department.

That made his siblings and him, in some people's eyes, related to the reigning royalty.

It also made them, Shane was quickly learning, targets for verbal potshots.

While one of his brothers took each remark and the person who made it to task, Shane's method was to ignore the sarcastic sentiment and move on as if he hadn't heard it.

Eventually, he reasoned, those who felt compelled to make these remarks would get tired of the game and turn their attention elsewhere.

At least he could hope.

"I'll get right on it," Shane told the captain as he grabbed the jacket he had slung over the back of his chair and walked out of the squad room.

Getting on the elevator, he glanced at the note again and shook his head. He could barely make out all the words written on the paper. The captain had the handwriting of an illiterate gorilla—as well as the same physique, he added silently.

But he had managed to get the gist of it, although he *still* had no idea why someone attached to Animal Control would be calling in and asking for backup unless they'd encountered a pack of roving coyotes or something along those lines. Even in that case, wouldn't this Officer St. James have called his own department? Why had he called this in to Dispatch, which then had decided to route the call to Major Crimes?

And why hadn't the captain questioned this instead of passing it on to him?

Oh well, Shane thought with a careless shrug as he got out on the ground floor. He was happier in the field than sitting at his desk, staring down that mountain of paperwork.

Paperwork had always been the bane of his existence. It reminded him too much of homework, something he'd never really been good at. He'd always been a doer, not a recorder.

Locating his vehicle, Shane opened the dark sedan's driver's-side door and slid in behind the steering wheel. He buckled up, then, glancing into the rearview mirror, pulled out of the parking space.

He didn't need to wait for anyone. He was checking this out on his own.

It still felt a little strange to be going anywhere without Wilson riding shotgun, smelling faintly of

Old Spice and onions, going on ad nauseam about some recipe he'd seen prepared on one of the cable cooking channels that he was eager to try.

The only thing Wilson liked better than cooking was eating—which could account for why the man had no life outside the department, Shane mused. But Wilson had recently been approached about a transfer to Narcotics because they had a shortage of detectives in that section after two of their detectives had retired and another one had relocated to Dallas. He'd been debating saying yes when he'd been shot by a thief whose path they had accidentally crossed.

That had had not just one repercussion, but two. He'd temporarily lost his partner—and permanently lost his fiancée.

Better to find out now than later, he told himself not for the first time.

It still didn't help.

Wilson would be back on his feet soon enough, Shane thought. Right now, he was going to just enjoy the fact that he was unencumbered in the car and that no one was chattering nonstop about the "rare herbs and spices" he'd used to prepare some exotic recipe and coaxing him to sample something that appeared better suited to a landfill than a plate.

Shane got to the apartment complex in less than ten minutes. The ambulance had beaten him.

Because there appeared to be no parking spot readily available in what was designated as guest parking, and all the regular spaces corresponding to the apartments were already filled, Shane decided to park his sedan behind the police department's Animal Control truck. He had little use for people attached to the department who spent their days picking up roadkill.

A crowd was beginning to gather right outside the ground-floor apartment the captain had scribbled down on the paper.

"This must be the place," Shane said to himself. Getting out of his vehicle, he crossed to the first patrolman he saw and issued an order. "Keep these people back until we know what we're dealing with. Can't have them trampling all over what might be part of the crime scene."

The patrolman, a veteran of the department for twenty-two years, laughed softly to himself as he muttered under his breath. "Too late," Shane heard him say as he was about to walk away.

Since his father, Sean, was the head of the day shift's Crime Scene Investigation unit, Shane was exceedingly mindful of the preservation of any and all evidence that might pertain to the crime under investigation.

"What's that supposed to mean?" He wanted to know.

Rather than apologize or retract his comment, the officer explained his remark. "Dog's been running through everything."

Shane scowled, looking around the immediate area outside the apartment in question.

"What dog?" he asked. Before the officer could say a word, the incessant barking began again.

The officer Shane had confronted winced. "That dog," he answered, pointing at the open door and into the apartment.

Taking a step to the side, Shane peered in and was stunned. The dog, so boisterous just seconds ago, had stopped barking. Instead of running around the way the patrolman seemed to indicate he'd been doing, the animal was now safely and silently in the arms of what appeared to be a policewoman.

Leaving the patrolman to herd the onlookers back behind the barricades that had been put up, Shane walked into the apartment to look around.

There was an absolute maze of red paw prints zigzagging all over the faded beige carpeting in the living room and the cracked vinyl kitchen floor.

Apparently the policewoman hadn't been nearly fast enough scooping up the neurotic canine. It was obvious that the terrier had run through the victim's pool of blood more than just a few times.

Someone from his father's department was there already, taking copious photographs. The clicking shutter was just so much background noise as Shane made his way over to the body on the floor.

For the first time since he'd joined the force, Shane came dangerously close to revisiting his breakfast. The gaping wound in the woman's abdomen was almost surreal.

No one could lose this amount of blood and live,

he thought. He touched the side of her neck just to be sure. There was no pulse.

"This woman doesn't need a bus any longer. She belongs to the medical examiner now." Looking closer, he saw there was something about the way the blood was smeared on one side that didn't look right to him. His field of expertise was mainly white-collar crime, but he knew a bit about blood patterns, thanks to his father. "Who moved the body?" He wanted to know.

"I did."

The answer came from his right. Turning, Shane found himself looking at the officer who was holding the terrier. For the first time, as he focused on her, he realized that the perky-looking policewoman was covered with blood herself. Lots of blood. More, he thought, than he would have expected from someone checking out the crime scene.

"Why did you move her?" he asked.

"I thought she was only wounded," Ashley explained. "I didn't realize that someone had cut out her baby."

His eyes narrowed. Aurora was supposed to be this peaceful little city. What the hell was going on? He studied the woman in front of him. "You saying she was pregnant?"

Ashley nodded. As the dog began to whimper, she rocked slightly to soothe the animal in the same fashion a mother would rock to soothe a cranky child.

"Yes."

Was there more going on here than he'd thought? "Did you know her?"

Using small concentric circles to pet the animal she held against her, the policewoman shook her head. "No."

Had she just gotten caught in a lie? "Then how did you know she was pregnant?"

"First thing that came to mind when I saw the nature of the wound," she responded. "And then there were her final words—"

"She was alive when you first saw her?" he asked, surprised.

Ashley couldn't figure out if the detective was mocking her or if he just didn't have any people skills. For now, she gave him the benefit of the doubt.

"That's why I called for an ambulance," she told him. "I tried to stop the blood."

She was supposed to be a professional, Ashley told herself. After all, it wasn't as if she'd never seen blood before, or been around something that was dying or already dead. But what had gone down here this morning had her feeling as if she was walking in labored slow motion through a nightmare. A nightmare she should be able to wake up from.

"That would explain the jacket," he commented, glancing down at the blood-soaked article of clothing. "As well as the bloodstains on your knees." He looked at her for a long moment, then asked, "Where were you again this morning?"

There was no "again." He hadn't asked that question, Ashley thought. What was he trying to do here?

"I went to work this morning. My lieutenant gave me this address, said a complaint had been lodged about a dog in the apartment that wouldn't stop barking. The caller said the dog had been barking off and on for several hours."

Shane nodded at the almost docile dog in her arms. "That dog?"

Without fully realizing it, she closed her arms protectively around the animal. "Yes."

"Seems pretty quiet to me," he observed.

Ashley continued stroking the dog. "I have a way with animals. Besides, I think he's emotionally tired out."

He watched as she continued to stroke the dog. The animal seemed to be leaning into her, as if he thought he was safe.

"'Emotionally tired out'?" Shane repeated rather skeptically.

His tone, she judged, was intended to get her to back away from her observation. She didn't. "That's what I said."

"Dogs have emotions." It wasn't a question so much as a mocking statement.

Ashley forced herself to bite back a few choice words about the barely veiled sarcasm in his voice. She had a feeling that challenging the detective would only result in his becoming confrontational.

Nonetheless, she stood her ground. “All animals have emotions,” she informed him coolly.

“I’ll keep that in mind and try not to hurt his feelings,” he said, nodding at the terrier. Then his eyes shifted toward her. “Where were you before you came into work?”

Her eyes met his. She refused to look away. Only guilty people avoided eye contact. “Home.” She said the word almost defiantly.

“Can anyone verify that?” he asked.

There hadn’t been anyone to verify anything about her since she was four. For most of her life, until she’d turned eighteen, she had just blended into the woodwork or been invisible to the people around her.

“I’ve got two dogs, but they tend not to talk too much to strangers.” And then her flippant tone evaporated as she demanded, “Do you seriously think I had something to do with this?”

From where he stood, it wasn’t all that far-fetched, and until he had more details or knew otherwise, the woman made for a pretty decent suspect.

“A lot of times,” he told her, “the first one on the scene turns out to be the perp.”

Oh, come on, puh-lease! “What is that?” she asked. “A direct quote from *Murder for Dummies?*”

He did *not* care for her sarcastic tone. “You’ve got a smart mouth on you, you know that?” he challenged.

“Goes with the rest of me,” she replied with a

careless shrug, as if to shrug off his entire statement and whatever off-the-wall theory he was spinning. Shifting the terrier to her other side, much like a mother would shift the toddler she was holding, Ashley asked him, "Are you really a Homicide detective?"

"I'm from the Major Crimes Division," he revealed. "When you called Dispatch, you asked for backup and a bus," he reminded her.

"That was because I wasn't sure what was going on, and she was still breathing." Seemed to her that they had already gone over this and established it.

"Which was why you moved the body," he concluded.

This again, she thought, exasperated. What was this detective's problem? "I just turned her so she was on her back. I found her facedown on the floor between the kitchen and the living room. I didn't think to take a photo before I tried to find a way to save her life."

A key phrase in her statement stuck out for him, and Shane commented on it. "Apparently you didn't think at all." Before she could retort, he asked another question. "When you got here, was the door opened?"

"No," she told him, reciting the words stoically, "it was locked."

He looked around for another person besides the precinct personnel, but there was no civilian in the apartment. "Then the landlord let you in." It was an assumption on his part.

The next moment, the assumption was shot down as she answered, "No, he didn't."

His eyes narrowed. This wasn't adding up—unless she was the perpetrator. "Then how did you get in?" he asked.

Hadn't he noticed the pane of glass on the ground under the kitchen window? "I jimmied the kitchen window until I got a pane off."

He was going to give her every chance—before she hung herself. "Why would you—?"

Anticipating his question, Ashley had her answer ready. "I heard the dog barking, and I looked in through the window. That was when I saw the victim lying facedown on the floor. I called it in and went to get the guy in the leasing office, but the office was empty. Whoever was on duty was out, showing a potential tenant one of the apartments."

"So you jimmied the window and let yourself in."

He sounded as if he was accusing her. He couldn't be serious—could he?

"Yes, I jimmied the window and let myself in." She was truly annoyed. "Tell me, Detective, what would you have done?" she demanded angrily.

Chapter 3

For a moment the detective said nothing and Ashley thought he was going to give her hell for talking to him that way. She braced herself for a dressing down. It wouldn't be the first time she'd had one. Because there was no one else for her to turn to, she'd learned how to be her own person and to follow both her instincts and her conscience.

But when the detective finally did say something, he surprised her.

"I would've kicked in the door." Seeing the stunned look on her face, Shane smiled and explained, "I'm too big to fit in through that window."

It was the first time since he'd arrived that she'd seen even a hint of a smile on his lips. Until now, he'd been scowling at her. When he smiled, the detective looked, she thought, like a completely different person. He looked approachable, not to mention rather good-looking.

Not that what the man looked like really mattered one way or another, Ashley told herself—except for the fact that it was the good-looking ones who were usually also the pompous ones.

"Then it's lucky for you that she got here first. Those doors don't kick in as easily as you might think, Detective Cavanaugh. That's a fire door, and they're pretty damn sturdy. They only get 'kicked down' in movies and TV shows," a deep voice coming from directly behind her said amicably.

Ashley turned to see a tall, handsome older man walking in. He was carrying a rather formidable leather case with him. The letters *CSI* were embossed across the side of it.

Apparently seeing that she was looking at his case, the newcomer told her, "I'm with the crime lab." Ashley found it rather unusual that the investigator would tell her that rather than the detective, then realized that most likely, the detective had already been acquainted with the crime scene investigator.

Extending his hand to her, the man introduced himself. "I'm Sean Cavanaugh."

She flashed a smile at him, grateful to be treated as a person. A great many people on the force acted as if she was part of the scenery—inconsequential scenery, at that. That went along with the fact that there were those in the police department who viewed the people in her division as being no more than just glorified dog catchers.

She had a feeling, judging by the look on the detective's face when he'd first talked to her, that he thought the same.

But not this man, Ashley decided.

"Officer Ashley St. James," she responded, shaking his hand.

The man smiled at her. When he did, it occurred to her that he seemed to have the same kind of smile as the detective. Odd.

"Nice to meet you, Officer St. James." Placing his case on the coffee table, he opened it and took out his camera. He raised an eyebrow as he appeared to study her for a moment. "This your first murder?"

"Yes, sir, it is." And then she relaxed just a touch and asked, "It shows, huh?"

The reply he gave wasn't one she was expecting.

"As a matter of fact, it doesn't." Sean began to snap pictures of anything in the room that might fit under the heading of possible evidence. "That's why I asked. You seem remarkably composed for someone who's seen something this gruesome." He looked over his shoulder at the detective. "Doesn't she, Shane?"

Shane had no idea why his father would attempt to get a three-way conversation going in the middle of something so horrendous as this murder—unless it was his way of helping the little officer cope with what she'd stumbled across.

Now that he thought about it, that sounded *exactly* like something his father would do. He was always in there, the voice of calm and reason, trying to help people through a rough patch.

His father was probably the finest man he knew, Shane thought, not for the first time.

"Yeah, composed," Shane repeated. Let his father take care of whatever support the officer holding the dog might need. He wasn't here to hold her hand, pretty as it might be, he was here to try to figure out who killed the young woman on the floor—and why.

"He's usually a lot more talkative than that," Sean told her, leaning in and making the comment sound somehow confidential. He took a fourth shot of the victim from yet another angle. "Aren't you, Shane?"

"If you say so," he responded carelessly as he squatted over the victim to take a closer look.

The terrier the officer was holding became agitated and started barking. The bark grew more aggressive. Shane rose, his expression reverting to the annoyed look he'd worn for the initial part of their exchange. "Can't you get that dog out of here?"

"Not yet," she answered, stroking the small canine. She leaned over and whispered something in its ear just before she reached into her pocket and took out one of the treats she kept with her at all times. Bribed, the dog calmed somewhat and stopped barking.

Still petting the animal, Ashley looked from the crime scene investigator to the detective. The latter hadn't bothered to introduce himself. He'd gone straight to work and was treating her as if she were a suspect. Her eyes shifted back again. The more she compared the two, the more similarities she saw.

"Are you two related, by any chance?" she asked the older man, since he was definitely the friendlier one. "You kind of look alike."

Sean laughed to himself as he went on working. "Thank you, Officer. I'm sure Shane thinks of himself as the better looking one."

Her eyes narrowed slightly as she studied both men again, this time very carefully. They had the same cheekbones, the same strong jaws and the same eye color, she realized. Most likely, when he was younger, the crime scene investigator had probably had the same color hair as the detective.

"He's your son," she concluded.

"On good days," Sean acknowledged with a nod. "On bad days, he's his mother's."

His son hadn't given her his name. He was somewhat surprised at the omission. Had something caught Shane's attention, something that made him forget to follow the usual procedure? "You didn't tell her who you are?" Sean asked his son.

It was Ashley who answered him, shaking her head. "He went straight to questioning me," she told Sean. "Said something about the first one on the scene being a good suspect for the murder."

Sean glanced at his son. His expression was hard to read.

"Be gentle with him," Sean told the young officer. He winked at her, then picked up his case. He began to head toward the back of the apartment and the victim's bedroom. "This is his first murder, too."

That might explain why he was so stiff, Ashley thought. Still holding the terrier in her arms, she turned toward the investigator's son. "Will you be needing me, Detective Cavanaugh?"

The sun was finally pushing its way into the apartment through the rear sliding-glass doors, lighting the corners of the room that had previously been hidden in the shadows.

It also seemed to weave itself through the petite officer's red hair, giving it highlights and making it shine alluringly. Catching his attention, it caused Shane's train of thought to halt abruptly.

Beautiful women always caught his attention, and whatever else this woman was, she was definitely beautiful.

"What?" he asked, realizing that she'd said something and was waiting for an answer. Preoccupied, he didn't have a clue as to what she'd just asked.

"Will you be needing me?" she repeated, then added, "Any further?"

Ashley had lost her train of thought because the detective was looking at her rather intently, as if he was weighing something.

It took effort for her not to shift uncomfortably.

"You have a card on you, Officer?" he finally asked, his eyes holding hers. "You never know when that need might come up."

She knew she had to be misinterpreting his words, but the last part sounded much too personal, almost intimate. She could feel her cheeks warming, turning a different shade than they'd been just a moment ago. He'd worded his explanation just ambiguously enough to make it sound as if he might want her for something other than verbal input.

Not for the first time, she cursed her fair complexion. It was a dead giveaway.

Ashley forced herself to calm down and regain control over at least her outward appearance.

This one, she decided, fancied himself a ladies' man, someone who probably wasn't accustomed to being refused. Taking a card with her name on it out of her pocket, she handed it to him and answered, "No, I guess you just never do."

Turning on her heel, she started for the door.

"You taking that dog to the shelter?" he called out after her.

He honestly didn't know why he'd asked that. He really didn't care where the animal went, as long as it didn't run through the crime scene again.

"Why?" she asked, slipping a shielding hand around the terrier as if to silently communicate to the animal that it had no reason to fear anything as long as it was under her protection. "You want to question him later and rule him out as a suspect, too?"

The woman's feisty attitude intrigued him even as it annoyed him. "I want to tie up all the ends I can in my report. That includes where the dog was relocated. Now can I put down that he was taken to the animal shelter where he can be found until the city disposes of him."

He'd used the phrase to cover all bases—if the dog went on to be adopted by someone looking for a pet, it was considered to be one method of "disposal." But even so, she didn't care for the detective's cold, detached manner.

"You can put down anything you want, Detective Cavanaugh. But if you must know, I'll be taking the dog home with me when my shift is over." It was a spur of the moment decision on her part and it wasn't exactly according to the rules—but that was how she got the other two dogs she currently shared her house with. Animal Control's rules were slightly bendable, allowing her some leeway.

The way there apparently wasn't in the main division, she observed.

Shane looked from the dog in her arms to her. "Why would you do that?"

Ashley continued to pet the dog as she spoke. "Because he's been traumatized enough for one day, and I thought he could do with calm, tranquil surroundings for a while. He can't receive that sort of attention if I take him to Animal Control. We don't have enough personnel available for that."

Shane looked at her skeptically. He didn't know what to make of this woman. Was she some PETA-type radical in uniform, or just a pushover—at least where animals were concerned?

"Isn't giving him individualized care a little over the top?" he asked.

Ashley lifted her chin defiantly. "It shouldn't be," she informed him.

Shane laughed shortly. "Easy to see why the dog likes you so much."

"Why?" she asked, curious about the kind of reasoning he was using—and bracing herself for the worst.

Shane assumed that would be crystal clear to her. Was she fishing for a compliment? "Because you're taking his side, speaking up for him."

Maybe she was taking sides with the dog, but there was something about this detective that made her want to instantly take the opposite side of whatever he said.

"I just balance out the people who get off on kicking dogs," she replied simply.

The expression on his face shifted to one of amusement. "Are you a crusader, Officer St. James?"

She squared her shoulders, subconsciously bracing for a fight. She didn't like being laughed at. "Not a crusader," she answered. "Just someone doing her job the way she sees fit. Now, if you're finished with us, Detective, I'll take Albert out of here."

"'Albert,'" he repeated, surprised. "You know the dog's name?"

Evidently he was thinking that if she knew that—given there was no dog tag on the animal—she had to know the victim, as well.

"No, but he looks like an Albert," Ashley answered, shifting her hands and holding the dog up as if she was examining all sides of him, mimicking the process she'd employed when deciding on his name.

"If you say so," the detective murmured under his breath.

"Oh, Officer," Sean Cavanaugh called as he stepped out of the bedroom for a moment. "Before I forget, we'll need to check out that terrier. We might find something in his fur that'll tell us something about the person who did this. I can have one of my people take him over to Animal Control when we're done."

Ashley looked down at the dog. She could feel the animal begin to tremble against her, as if he actually understood what was being said and knew he was about to be separated from her.

"If you don't mind, I'd like to take him. He doesn't really look as if he trusts any of you."

She knew her request wasn't according to protocol, but had sensed that the elder Cavanaugh might not be a stickler for the letter of the rules, just the spirit.

"That would be fine," he told her, "as long as you

take him in right now. I can't have any possible evidence being contaminated."

"Understood," she replied, then flashed a smile intended strictly for the senior Cavanaugh. "I'm on my way," she announced, leaving.

For a moment Shane watched the woman leave with the canine she was protecting.

The second she walked out the door, he turned toward his father—only to find that he had retreated into the bedroom. Shane was quick to make his way to the back of the apartment.

Having the case land in his lap like this seemed almost serendipitous because lately he'd been thinking about asking to be transferred to the homicide division. Homicide was where all the up-and-comers wanted to go, so why shouldn't he?

Walking into the bedroom, he saw another crime scene investigator in the room with his father, collecting physical evidence. Probably the same man his father had intended to have transport the terrier to the lab before the officer had volunteered to do it.

Shane nodded at the man then planted himself in front of his father, waiting until Sean was finished with whatever he was doing.

Looking up, his father noted his presence and went back to photographing the bedroom.

"Cute," he pronounced out of the blue.

"What is?" Shane asked.

Sean looked up at him as if to ask, "Are you kidding me?" But he obliged his son by spelling it all out for him. "That officer with the material witness in her arms."

Shane shrugged his shoulders carelessly. "If you like that sort of thing," he agreed.

The deliberate nonchalant reply had Sean looking up at his son. "You *always* like that sort of thing," Sean reminded him. "At least, you used to," he amended.

For the past eight months, his son had been engaged to be married—until she'd broken it off last month after his partner had been shot on the job. For a while, it had been touch and go for Shane, but after what he'd just witnessed, Sean felt that his son was definitely on his way to recovery.

"Not when they're mouthy," Shane countered.

Sean was really intrigued now. "She's a challenge. Good, you could use one. And cute or not, the ladies are always far more interesting when they don't just fall at your feet in complete surrender. I noticed that you used to lose interest when women looked at you with those puppy-dog eyes."

Shane shrugged. All he wanted now was a good time. Getting serious just led to complications he didn't want anymore. "What's wrong with that?"

"There's no lightning, no lasting attraction," his father pointed out. "Where's the fun in that?"

"I'd tell you, but I'm not sure you're old enough to hear that kind of stuff."

Sean saw through his son's words and his attempt

at diverting him. "Is this one getting to you?" he asked.

The grin faded as Shane's expression became deadly serious. "Why would you say that?"

"Because instead of shrugging off what I say, you're making denials, protesting. That usually means only one thing—"

"Okay," Shane said, cutting him off. "This is me shrugging. Watch." He raised and lowered his wide shoulders in an exaggerated fashion.

But Sean wasn't buying any of it. "Too late for that," he told his son.

"Too late for *what?*" Shane demanded, completely at a loss as to where this complicated conversation was actually headed.

The look in Sean's eyes all but shouted, "You know, the die has already been cast, my boy." Out loud, Sean said, "Go, observe. Be a detective. Detect."

Shane shook his head. Ever since his father had gotten married again, to the mother of his sister's fiancée, he seemed determined for all of his offspring to be harnessed in a similar tether. Well, that might work for the others—it seemed as if everyone except for himself and Declan, his brother, seemed to be dropping like flies at the marriage altar—but he'd tried to go that route and gotten kicked in the teeth by cupid. Life had decreed that he was going to remain single, just like Declan. Currently, in their immediate family, they were the last two men standing.

He intended to remain "standing" for a very long time to come.

Putting his father and his father's less-than-subtle hints out of his head, Shane looked around the bedroom. Aside from a small bureau and a double bed, every other stick of furniture and random item in the room all but shouted baby.

This woman had been getting ready for her unborn child.

He couldn't help but feel sorry for the dead woman. The next moment he upbraided himself. Feeling sorry for the woman wasn't going to help solve the case. He was going to have to work at hardening his reaction if he hoped to get a permanent transfer to Homicide.

Donning a pair of disposable gloves, Shane carefully handled the contents of a fancy shopping bag. The bag was light blue on one side, light pink on the other. The words *Baby Mine* were written in fancy lettering on both sides.

"It's an expensive baby boutique," Sean told him when he noticed him staring at the bag.

Shane looked at him, puzzled. That was an odd piece of information for a man his father's age to have. "How would you know that?"

"I know a lot of things," Sean answered, amused at his son's attitude. "I don't just go home at the end of the day and crawl into a shell, pulling the door closed after myself."

Shane shrugged. "I just figured that things like

babies and all the stuff that goes with them are way in your past by now."

Sean glossed over the comment about his age. "Maybe so, but grandkids aren't."

It took a second for his father's words to replay themselves in his head. At that point, it was as if his brain did a double-take. "What grandkids?" he asked.

"Show up a little more often at those Sunday dinners your uncle Andrew likes to throw, and maybe you'll find out," Sean told him mysteriously.

It still felt strange calling someone he'd grown accustomed to knowing as the former chief of police his uncle. It was going to take more getting used to, he thought—just like his last name. Half the time he still wanted to say "Cavelli" when he introduced himself for the first time to someone.

"I've shown up at a few," Shane told his father defensively.

"Show up at a few more," his father countered, then, glancing up, he waved him off. "You're in my light, Shane."

Shane stepped to the side, narrowly avoiding bumping into a pile of stuffed animals, all still with their price tags on.

He picked one up to look over. Since he was wearing latex gloves, he couldn't feel the toy's furry texture, but he had a feeling that it was exceedingly soft. He shook his head as he put the stuffed animal back, feeling exceptionally sorry for the victim again.

"It looks like she was really looking forward to being a mother," he commented to his father.

"Yes, she was," Sean agreed.

Shane shook his head over the waste of it all. "Shame she's never going to get the chance."

Sean agreed with his son completely. "Make it up to her."

He didn't even know the victim. Just how was he supposed to do something like that?

"And just how do you propose I do that, seeing the woman's present condition?" he asked his father.

"Catch her killer," Sean said simply.

"Right." With a nod, Shane left the bedroom. He had just caught his very first homicide case, he thought, still trying to get used to the idea.

He needed to get busy.

Chapter 4

"Sorry about the accommodations."

Ashley directed her apology over her shoulder. It was for the four-footed passenger riding inside the van portion of her police vehicle. With slots located on all four sides to allow for the flow of air into the rear of the official vehicle, she knew that Albert could hear her voice, and hopefully, it would calm him down a bit.

At the moment, though, she could hear the dog moving around all four corners of the area that was accessible to him. He was obviously looking for a way out, an escape from his confinement.

"They just want to make sure that you don't have anything embedded in your fur that might have been accidentally left behind by your mistress's killer."

Easing to a stop at the crosswalk as she waited for the light to turn green, she turned her head so that her voice would carry to the rear of the van. "And they probably want to swab your paws, too, even though you did do a lot of running around. The problem is that you ran through that poor woman's blood, you know."

In response to her low-key voice, she heard the animal continue to whine. And maybe it was her imagination, but he did seem to slow down a little—or at least he didn't seem to be bouncing off the walls of the van as much as he initially had.

"I'll be with you the entire time," she promised the terrier. "And I'm not sure exactly what they're planning on doing in the way of taking evidence, but I do know that it's going to be totally painless. I promise," Ashley added.

Mindful of the stressed-out animal, she kept up a steady, low, soothing monologue for the entire trip back to the precinct.

Once there, she parked in a completely different area than she ordinarily did when she returned the vehicle for the night. Rather than the hidden side lot, she turned her vehicle in toward the much larger front lot. The front entrance was closer to the elevator she needed to use to get to the crime scene unit's lab. The entire facility was located in the basement of the building.

"We're here," she announced to the terrier as she opened the van's rear door.

The second she did, the red-pawed terrier tried to bolt out of his temporary prison. Acting on instinct, Ashley made a quick grab for the animal's dark green collar. Her quick reflexes caught the dog off guard and he wound up tripping over his own paws, falling backward.

She winced as she felt the poor dog's unfortunate jolt telegraph itself through her arm.

"Now you see, if you just took it easy, that wouldn't happen. Are you all right?" she asked, taking the small animal into her arms. He resisted at first, then seemed to surrender again, leaning against her and taking some solace from her warmth. "See? Much better, right?"

"You always talk to things that can't answer you?"

Startled, she swung around only to find the detective she'd left behind in the apartment walking up to her. How had he gotten here so fast, and why was he so intent on harassing her?

"Number one, it's a dog—a living, breathing entity—not a thing," she pointed out. "And number two, there are ways to communicate other than talking."

"He's communicating with you via mental telepathy now?" Shane asked, not bothering to hide the amused, mocking note in his voice.

"Like with people," she stubbornly pointed out, "a dog's actions tell me a great deal about what he's feeling."

This was growing more and more unbelievable to him. Was this petite fireball really serious?

"So now we're dealing with a dog's feelings?" he asked sarcastically.

Instead of answering the detective's question, Ashley had one of her own to ask him. "Don't you have some suspect to harass, or some clues to follow up on? I wouldn't want to take you away from your important work, Detective."

"Right now, the best clues might very well be on that ill-tempered dog you're holding on to," he informed her glibly. And then he became serious. "Why don't you drop off the mutt in the lab downstairs, and then I'll take your official statement?"

She had no intention of complying since she'd already decided on another path. "Number one, Albert's not a mutt, he's a Jack Russell terrier."

"Whatever." He shrugged it off. To him, dogs came in just three varieties. Small dogs, medium dogs and large dogs.

"Number two, I have an alternate suggestion for you. How about I take Albert to the lab, have them do their tests and then, when they're finished with him, I'll come back and talk to you afterward."

"Are you just trying to be difficult?" he asked.

The way she saw it, she was doing her best to be cooperative. "I promised Albert that I wouldn't leave him alone at the lab." And then she smiled innocently at Shane. "Making things difficult for you is just an added bonus."

"You *promised* Albert," he repeated incredulously, fairly certain—although, given who he was dealing with, he wasn't positive—that she *had* to be kidding.

"Yes. And I don't want him not to trust me," she told him. She could tell by his expression what Cavanaugh thought of that, but then, the detective really wasn't her first concern. The traumatized dog was. "If I break my word, Albert will just become that much harder to deal with."

He stared at her, stunned. "Do you actually believe what you are saying?"

So now he was accusing her of making things up as she went along? "Of course I do," she answered firmly. "Why wouldn't I?"

"Because," he responded, "for one thing, you make that mutt sound as if he had more intelligence than the average person."

"I told you, he's not a mutt," she informed him tersely. "He's a Jack Russell terrier, and as for having more intelligence than the average person, he probably does." She punctuated her statement with a toss of her head. This man obviously knew *nothing* about dogs. "Jack Russell terriers are extremely intelligent canines. They're also rather temperamental—" she shot Shane an accusing look "—also like some people I know."

Shane let her walk to the building entrance ahead of him, then reached around her to hold the door open for her. He saw the suspicious look that immediately crossed her face.

The woman probably thought he was trying to make a move on her.

"Don't worry, I'm just holding the door open for you, Officer St. James, nothing else. Speaking of being trusting, you're not, are you?" Shane asked, his eyes meeting hers.

Ashley met his scrutinizing glance head-on just before she walked into the main lobby. "No, I'm not."

He took a guess at the most logical reason she'd be distrusting. "What happened, you found out your boyfriend was cheating on you?"

There was no way she was about to let him know a single personal thing about her life. "I just haven't found people in general to be trustworthy," she replied coolly. "That's why I like animals better. They don't lie."

There was something about the way she said it that caught Shane's attention. He found his curiosity aroused. "Who lied to you, St. James?"

Her eyes narrowed. He could tell that it took everything she had not to tell him to butt out, that her personal life was none of his business. Instead, she apparently decided to play along. "Do you want that chronologically, alphabetically or arranged by height?"

He assumed she was just exaggerating, but there was no way he was going to accuse her of that. "Ouch, that many?"

"That many," she confirmed, her expression remaining impassive.

Ignoring the detective, Ashley was about to sweep past the front desk and head directly to the elevator.

"Hold on a minute," the sergeant manning the front desk called out. He looked uncertainly at the terrier in her arms and directed his question to Ashley. "Shouldn't you be using the rear entrance, heading toward Animal Control with that mutt?" He nodded his head toward the terrier.

She could actually *feel* Cavanaugh's grin as the sergeant referred to Albert as a mutt, just as he had. She ignored him.

At the sound of the new voice, the terrier became agitated and began to bark again.

"Shh, it's okay, Albert," she whispered softly to the dog before answering the sergeant. "I'm supposed to take him down to the crime lab."

Shane intervened. "It's okay, Murphy, she's with me."

She looked at Shane, surprised by his statement. "No, I'm not," she contradicted.

"I'm taking you to the crime lab," Shane informed her. "So that makes you with me."

"I can find it on my own," she retorted. "So that makes me with *me*."

He looked at her for a long moment, then took a guess. "Ever been there before?"

She didn't see what that had to do with it. It was just another department in the building. "No, but—"

"I have," he said, cutting her off. "I'll be your guide."

Exactly how incompetent did he think she was? "It's in the basement," she pointed out, "not somewhere in the Northwest Territory, Sacagawea. I think I can find where I'm supposed to go."

Shane laughed, as if that was a common mistake almost everyone made. "Trust me, it's better with a guide," he told her, taking hold of Ashley's arm. The moment he did, the dog began to growl. Rather than pull back his hand, Shane just scowled at the animal. "You want to call him off?" It was more of a command than a question.

Which was exactly why Ashley bristled at his tone. "I think it might just be simpler for him if you let go of my arm."

For a moment Shane debated standing his ground, but it hardly seemed worth it. So after a beat—just not to seem as if he was jumping through hoops—he removed his hand from her arm. "Have it your way."

He found the half smile that rose to her lips irritating and yet oddly intriguing at the same time. Intriguing even though he'd made a silent promise to himself that he wasn't going to even remotely approach this no-man's land for a very long time to come.

Not until after he'd fully recovered from what Kitty had done, and most likely, not even then.

The way he saw it, one sliced-up ego was enough for any man to deal with in one lifetime.

Granted, he'd never had to go through something like this before, but when it happened, it had caught him so completely off balance, it had taken not just his very breath away, it had also taken away a great deal of his inner confidence.

"Thanks for your 'permission,' Detective," Ashley retorted icily, "but I really don't need it."

He wasn't put off by her tone. Instead he looked at her very closely and asked, "Exactly what *do* you need, Officer?"

She raised her chin, and Shane caught himself thinking that it made one hell of a tempting target. A target that was almost *too* tempting to resist.

"Space," she informed him.

"Then you're out of luck at the moment," he informed her. "You won't find overly much of that downstairs," he answered. "In fact, it's more like one great big maze until you get used to it."

"And you're used to it." It wasn't a question; it was an assumption since he was offering to play the big safari guide. She couldn't see him making the offer if he had a tendency to get lost.

"Yeah."

The elevator finally arrived, and Ashley walked in first. He was right behind her.

Because of her upbringing—or more accurately, the lack of it, Ashley had learned to pick her battles. Otherwise, life became one huge battleground and after a while, she lost her perspective. That guaranteed her to be the major loser in any confrontation.

"Okay," she said as she pressed the button on the bottom. The doors closed, and the elevator began to go down.

"Okay what?" he challenged, waiting for her to be flippant or perhaps even painfully specific. He was beginning to learn that she wasn't as easily readable as he'd initially thought.

Rather than give him any kind of an answer he could understand, Ashley lifted one shoulder in a half shrug and said, "Just okay."

By the time she said that, the elevator had made the short trip from the first floor down to the basement. The silvery doors slid open. Eager to put any distance she could between them, Ashley hurried through the doors before they were even completely parted.

She looked around the immediate area. She hated to admit it, but Cavanaugh was right. It *did* look like a maze down here. A narrow maze that offered her two directions to go. Which way did she go? Neither wall was labeled to make it easy for anyone not intimately familiar with the lab's layout.

She looked at Shane, waiting for the detective to come through and tell her where the lab she needed to go to with Albert was located. After all, wasn't that the whole reason he'd said he was accompanying her to begin with?

Guessing what was going on in her head right now, Shane savored the moment. "Don't know which direction to take, do you?"

Wiping the smirk off a detective's face wouldn't be a good career move at this point of her life, Ashley thought darkly. Unlike the fine young detective, she didn't have a family name to fall back on or a well-placed superior to take up her side.

But God, removing that smirk from his lips would feel good.

Nevertheless, mindful of the consequences, she restrained herself and answered, "Eventually, there has to be a sign, but in the interest of not wasting your precious time watching me try to find it, why don't you just tell me which way to go?"

For two cents, he might, Shane couldn't help thinking. But that wasn't going to move this case along an inch—although it undoubtedly would be very soul-satisfying.

Nevertheless, when he pointed in response to her question, it was to the right. He wasn't about to plant a red herring or to play a practical joke on this less than jovial woman.

"That way."

Her "Thank you" in response was so cold, he thought he was in danger of getting frostbite despite the fact that it was just September, and they were in the middle of a Santa Ana condition. The devil winds were blowing in hot and merciless from the desert.

He kept a smile plastered on his lips as he replied, "Don't mention it."

Don't worry, I don't intend to do it more than once, she silently told him, keeping her arms wrapped around the terrier to afford the animal as much of a feeling of security as she could.

Too bad the terrier couldn't return the favor, she thought. She was definitely out of her element down here.

"Turn there," Shane instructed. "To your left," he added when she all but missed the small door that was on that side.

Grudgingly following his instruction, Ashley walked into the lab.

Unlike the corridor she'd just been down, the large rectangular room, outfitted with a myriad of strange-looking equipment and devices, was extremely well lit. All shadows had been summarily banished from this part of the basement.

Hearing a commotion behind her, the young woman in the lab coat turned from a mysterious machine she'd just inserted a test tube into.

Her serious expression instantly melted when she saw Shane. "Hi, Shane, what brings you here to my part of the world?" Her glance took in the dog as well as the young woman holding the animal. "And you brought me a visitor. Two," she amended, looking at the terrier. Her eyes rose to meet the woman's. "Hi, I'm Destiny Richardson," she said, introducing herself.

Of course you are, Ashley thought, offering a perfunctory smile.

It figured that he would have a girlfriend named Destiny, she couldn't help thinking as she watched the two of them interact. The lab technician probably fit right in with girls who had names like Bambi and Tiffany. Ashley was willing to bet those belonged to two more of his girlfriends.

"Ashley St. James," Ashley told the lab technician in response.

"And your friend?" Destiny asked, removing one latex glove to pet the terrier the officer was holding.

To Ashley's surprise, the terrier didn't instantly begin barking. Instead he allowed himself to be petted by this woman. He even seemed to like it, she realized. The woman went up several notches in her estimation. Maybe she wasn't just a bimbo after all.

"Albert," Ashley replied, then commented, "He seems to like you."

"Everyone likes Destiny," Shane interjected.

Destiny laughed softly. "That's only because I'm a lot happier these days than I used to be," she told Ashley modestly.

Next the woman would be batting her eyes at Cavanaugh and saying he was the reason behind the changes in her life, Ashley guessed.

It took everything she had not to just roll her eyes—or get nauseous. Had he come down here to guide her the way he'd claimed, or to flaunt one of his girlfriends at her?

As if she cared, Ashley thought.

"Maybe I should come back later?" she suggested. "Give you and...Destiny, is it—?" she asked, pretending not to have noted the technician's name "—a little alone time together."

Destiny looked at her, clearly more confused than Shane appeared.

"Why would we need any alone time together?" she questioned.

Shane was the one who answered her rather than the woman who'd initially made the offer. "I think that's the officer's quaint way of saying she thinks we're in a relationship."

Ashley scowled at Cavanaugh for the cavalier way he'd just volunteered her guess. He really did tick her off, and if anything, his good looks just seemed to intensify her annoyance.

But that slipped into the background the next moment when the sound of the lab technician's laughter told Ashley that maybe she'd made a mistake.

Chapter 5

"I'm sorry," Destiny apologized as she stopped laughing. "I guess I do look like a woman in love," she agreed. "But though Shane's a terrific guy and I do love him—" she nodded in the detective's direction "—I love him like a brother. Shane is *not* the object of my affections. His brother, Logan, is."

It was obvious by the look in her eyes that the woman was very, very much in love with whoever this Logan person was. Undoubtedly another Cavanaugh, Ashley assumed, since she'd just referred to Shane as his brother. The police department seemed to be absolutely *crawling* with them. The only one she actually knew was Dr. Patience Cavanaugh Coltrane. She was the vet who took care of the police dogs in the K-9 division, and she was really terrific, but that in no way reflected on the rest of the family.

When it came to accepting things, she'd always been a person who needed to be shown rather than told. She'd been burned too many times not to be that way.

"We're getting married soon," Destiny confided in what amounted to a stage whisper.

The moment the words were out of her mouth, a wave of regret washed over her. There was concern in her eyes as they darted toward Shane. "Oh, God, Shane, I am so sorry. I didn't mean to—"

Mindful of the officer standing between them, Shane was quick to cut his future sister-in-law off. "Nothing to be sorry about," he told her, absolving Destiny of any residual guilt. He cited the comparison she was making as one that compared apples and oranges, even though it really wasn't.

The concern did not leave Destiny's face. "How are you doing these days?" she asked.

"Great," Shane told her with feeling, as if volume could negate the sense that his heart had been turned into shredded wheat. "And I'll be even better once you examine this ill-tempered, four-footed barking machine and let me know if the little devil's carrying around any clues as to the identity of the person who murdered his poor mistress."

"What happened?" Destiny asked, needing to know the circumstances surrounding the case to help her determine what she should be looking for.

"Someone performed a very primitive C-section on his owner to steal her unborn child." It was Ashley who filled her in. Her own words caused her to shudder.

"Oh God," Destiny murmured, trying to distance herself from the gruesome image the officer's description created. She looked at the terrier the Animal Control officer was holding. "Did the dog bite the perpetrator?" she asked hopefully.

"We were kind of hoping you could tell us," Ashley told her.

For a second Destiny looked at what she was doing, then, making a spur of the moment decision, set the test tube aside and said, "Sure, I'll run some tests, see what we can find out. C'mon, boy," she said to the terrier, taking him from the other woman. "You and I have a date with a wide-tooth comb."

Shane watched, surprised that his future sister-in-law was not on the receiving end of a display of the canine's hyper temper.

"Why did he bark at me and not you?" he couldn't help wondering out loud. It wasn't as if he made a habit of abusing dogs and Albert had sensed it.

"Maybe he's a good judge of character," Ashley intoned. It earned her a rather dirty, exasperated look from the man beside her.

Shane decided that taking umbrage at her comment would wind up being a waste of time, so he put it out of his mind. "Why don't we go up to the squad room and you can give me that statement now?" he suggested instead.

Ashley looked toward the dog, now with Destiny in another part of the large lab. "I'd rather wait until she's finished with him, if you don't mind."

She'd said it politely enough, but he knew she wasn't asking for his indulgence. She was telling him she wasn't about to leave until the animal was leaving with her. This was carrying her duties to the extreme, he thought.

"If I leave, Albert might become agitated. But you can go," she told him cheerfully.

"Doesn't seem like much point in going up there to take your statement if you're not up there with me," he pointed out, enunciating each word.

She looked at him. Was he planning on waiting around with her? "Don't you have anything else to do?"

"No, I kinda wanted to solve this murder before noon," Shane answered in a deliberately saccharine voice. Then his tone changed as he said more seriously, "Yes, I've got other things to do, but the details of this murder take precedence over everything else at the moment."

"So, just to be clear, you're going to wait here in the lab with me until Destiny is finished checking Albert out?" she asked in disbelief.

He got the impression that she wasn't happy about that. Why? "Looks that way."

To Ashley, it also looked as if she was stuck. Well,

she might as well make the most of it. "Okay, answer a question for me."

He looked at her with a touch of wariness, wondering just what the woman was up to. Well, he wasn't going to find out by just staring at her. With a shrug, he said, "Go ahead."

"Why did Destiny apologize for being so happy about her upcoming wedding?" she asked. "It seems only natural that she would be."

Ashley knew that whatever was at the bottom of this was most likely a private matter, but she had to say that her curiosity had been aroused by the look of contrition on the lab technician's face. Why would a wedding matter to this irreverent detective? People were usually happy about a wedding taking place in the family.

At the same time that she was wondering about his reaction, Ashley told herself she was curious only because she liked having all her facts straight before her, not because the situation somehow intrigued her or actually mattered to her.

When the detective made no reply to her question, she took a guess. "Were the two of you together at some point?"

"At no point," Shane informed her tersely.

Despite his protest, had she hit a sensitive spot? "Then why?"

What was with all these questions? Shane made no effort to hide his annoyance. "Are you practicing being a detective?"

Not rising to the bait, she replied, "No, I'm just being human."

"Good luck with that," Shane snapped.

Damn it, he wasn't supposed to be this sensitive about it after all the time that had passed. He'd always been one to roll with the punches and then move along. But this particular turn of events, he had to admit, had definitely sucker punched him. He'd actually thought that what he and Kitty had had was something special, something that was going to last.

That he could be so wrong had thrown him and wreaked havoc on not just his confidence, but on his ability to make a judgment call.

He'd hurt her, Shane thought. He could see it flash across the officer's face before she quickly replaced the expression with an indifferent one. The woman was shutting down, he realized.

"Sorry," he muttered. Apologies did not come easily to him, but he owned up to his mistakes. "You didn't deserve that."

While apologies had never been her undoing, neither could she remain indifferent to someone who actually tendered one to her, apologizing for his insensitive comment. That hardly ever happened to her.

"No," she agreed, "I didn't." Ashley paused, obviously debating saying her next words, then deciding to go ahead. "You might want to work on your social skills when you start questioning people about this murder," she advised somewhat stiffly.

He'd never had problems with social skills. At

least, not before the breakup. He looked at Ashley for a long moment.

"I was engaged," Shane said out of the blue after a beat.

Ashley looked at him, picking up on the key word. "Was?"

Shane frowned. What did she need, a road map? "Yeah, was."

The two words just hung in the air, begging for a follow-up. Begging for something more substantial.

Since the detective wasn't volunteering anything, Ashley guessed that maybe he needed to be prodded in order to continue. Nobody just threw out that type of single sentence and then left it at that.

"What happened?"

He'd asked himself that a dozen times, examining the events as they'd occurred an equal amount of times. The answers he'd come up with were unacceptable—but they were all he had. "My partner got shot."

Ashley waited, but the detective didn't say anything further. With a sigh, she told him, "You're going to have to give me more of a clue than that. What did your partner getting shot have to do with your engagement breaking up?" Even as she asked, an answer occurred to her and her eyes darted in his direction. "You weren't engaged to your partner, were you?"

Rather than answer her directly, Shane stared off

into the distance as he relayed the incident. "When Vance got shot, Kitty said that she suddenly realized it could have been me in the hospital. Me in the morgue."

Her eyes widened as sympathy flooded through her. "Did your partner—?"

He'd anticipated her question. "No, he didn't die, but he could have. Kitty said she couldn't live with the uncertainty of not knowing from day to day if she was going to be a wife or a widow." His voice trailed off as he struggled to push the memory of the pain, of the feeling of being emotionally abandoned, away.

"Comes with the job," Ashley said simply.

He looked at her then. Why couldn't Kitty have seen it that way? Given half a chance, they could have been working on creating a family together by now.

"That's what I told her," he said quietly. "She wanted me to choose."

"Between the job and her?" If Ashley had been given that sort of a choice, she knew which she would have picked. Anyone who did that sort of thing to someone else didn't deserve to be chosen.

Shane shrugged. How the hell had they come to talking about this? "Yeah."

Well, he was here, so that answered the logical question as to which side he'd taken. "And you chose the job."

Shane laughed shortly, but this time his tone wasn't nasty as he said, "Nothing gets by you, does it?"

He was trying to be flippant, but she wasn't buying it. The man had been hurt. Deeply. And apparently, some members of his family or almost family felt he was *still* hurting.

"I'm sorry it didn't turn out, Cavanaugh."

"Yeah, me, too." And then he shrugged again. "Guess it just wasn't meant to happen. It probably would've fallen apart eventually, anyway."

"The marriage?" she asked, trying to get to the bottom of what he was telling her.

"Yeah."

Ashley wasn't following him. "What makes you say that?"

"Statistics," he answered tersely. When she continued looking at him quizzically, he elaborated. "Most detectives on the force are divorced once or twice. Some of them even more than that."

"Does that go for the Cavanaughs, too?" she asked him.

Like everyone else on the force, Ashley was aware of the family and the effect they had on the police force, but she didn't know all that much *about* them. For the most part, she kept to herself. That didn't really allow for much of anything to get into her world.

"Actually, no," he admitted. They were the flaw in his theory, but he didn't like to dwell on that. "As far as I can tell, Cavanaughs get married, and they stay married." But there was a basic reason for that, he thought. "A lot of them pick people who are part of law enforcement in some way. That gives them a leg up on all this."

"I take it your former fiancée wasn't part of our world." She saw the half smirk on Shane's face when she made the reference and correctly interpreted it. "Despite what you think of the division I work with, Animal Control *is* part of the police department."

The corners of his mouth curved. Granted, she was cute and feisty, but there was just no way to equate the two fields.

"Meet many armed possums during the course of your day, Officer?" he asked.

"My work isn't as tame as you seem to think it is," Ashley said defensively. "When was the last time you caught an injured pit bull that's just taken down a Doberman?" she challenged.

The closest he'd come to something like that was chasing down a bank robber who'd pulled a gun on him when he caught up to the man. If the gun hadn't jammed, he wouldn't have been here now—and Kitty's prophecy would have come true.

"You did that?" he asked, impressed.

She hadn't raised the example to garner any kind of recognition or bragging rights; she'd just wanted him to know that being in Animal Control wasn't just coasting along from day to day.

"With my heart in my throat, yes," she answered.

"How'd you do that?" he asked. "Catch the pit bull?" From what he knew about the breed, they were all teeth and bred for fighting. Without shooting it, the petite officer didn't stand a chance against one—most people didn't.

"All I can say is thank God for tranquilizing darts." She'd fired three into the charging animal, praying madly. "The pit bull stopped about a foot away from me." Half a second more and the dog's teeth would have ripped into her flesh.

Shane shook his head. Confronted with that, he might have quit the next day. Hell, that very afternoon. "That probably qualifies as the worst few minutes of your life."

Seemed it should. But it didn't, not with the kind of upbringing she'd had.

"That doesn't even make the top five."

The remark was out of her mouth before she could think to stop herself. She didn't even have to look at him to know that she'd captured the detective's attention.

Shane looked at her, suddenly seeing the petite woman in a completely different light. Just what sort of a life had she led? "What are the top five?"

"Sitting in the CSI lab, making small talk while waiting for the technician to finish fine-tooth-combing a Jack Russell terrier comes to mind."

He was beginning to realize that the woman blocked every attempt at delving into her life, or getting any answers. Why?

"I was being serious," he told her.

"So was I," she told him glibly.

Rising, Ashley crossed over to where Destiny was

presently running a comb through the animal's fur. "Are you almost finished?" she asked.

Destiny smiled placidly. "Almost." Glancing in her direction, Destiny's smile widened just a tad. "You're even more impatient than your furry friend here," she observed. "It'll take me another twenty minutes or so. Trust me," Destiny told her. "In the meantime, there's a pot of fresh coffee in the break room. I just made it," she added, then asked, "Why don't you help yourself to some?"

Ashley shook her head. "Thanks for the offer, but I don't drink coffee."

"'Don't drink coffee'?" Shane echoed. She turned to see that rather than remain seated, the detective had come up behind her.

Was this man going to shadow her every move all day long?

"That's almost un-American," he told her.

Since when was ingesting caffeine strictly the purview of the Americans?

"Be that as it may," she said, dismissing the detective's flippant observation. "I was forced to drink black coffee when I was a kid, and I developed a real distaste for it, so now that I don't have to drink coffee, I don't."

"'Forced'?" he repeated. "Who forced you to drink coffee?" He couldn't begin to imagine what sort of a parent would make their child drink something as strong as black coffee. What was wrong with them? Or did she have older siblings who'd thought it was fun to bully her any way they could find?

That was a poor choice of words on her part. She'd let it slip.

"That's not the point. The point is that I don't have to drink coffee, so I don't. But thank you for the thought," she said, addressing the lab technician.

Destiny nodded. "Almost done," she promised.

Shane said nothing as he studied the woman he'd thought of until just now as a glorified dog catcher. He'd promised himself that all he was going to do for the next year or so was just coast, enjoy himself and not take *any* of the fair sex seriously—no matter how attractive they turned out to be.

But despite his self-made promise, this woman he found himself temporarily allied with raised questions in his mind, questions that managed to intrigue him and draw him in at the same time.

She obviously didn't seem to want to volunteer anything personal about herself, at least not knowingly, but that only served to make him more curious and determined to find the answers.

Maybe what she needed was a more congenial atmosphere that was more conducive to sharing things.

"How about a drink?" he suggested.

Her eyes remained on the dog, as if she had a way of knowing the animal would sense if she was either preoccupied with something other than his well-being, or not here altogether.

"Excuse me?"

"Do you also not drink?" he asked. "I'm talking about stopping by Malone's after work and taking a social drink or two. Is that something you don't do, either?"

"Why, are you asking me out after work?" she asked.

Not in the sense that she meant—or at least, he didn't think he was—but who knew? Out loud he said, "Nothing wrong with grabbing a beer or something else if beer doesn't appeal to you."

"No," she agreed. "There's nothing wrong with it."

But she wasn't all that keen on it, either. She was waltzing around the elephant in the room, he thought. "So will you?"

She looked at him, leery. "With you?"

"And a room full of fellow officers," he added, in case she didn't trust him enough to be close to him without certain precautions. A crowd scene could afford her that kind of emotional protection.

"When was I promoted?" she asked him.

He didn't understand what she was getting at. "What?"

"Well, just a few minutes ago, I was a 'glorified dog catcher,'" she reminded him. "Now I'm suddenly a fellow officer."

"With one hell of a chip on your shoulder," he observed.

Her eyes met his defiantly. "Nothing I haven't earned, trust me."

"I'd like to," he told her with feeling, surprising Ashley. "I'll be there after my shift. Join me if you want to. Don't if you don't."

And that was all he said on the subject.

Chapter 6

"You keep watching that door as if you expect it to fly open any second and do tricks," Declan Cavanaugh observed, glancing over his shoulder at the tavern entrance.

"No, I'm not," Shane protested with what, even to his own ears, sounded like just a tad too much feeling.

It was obvious to him that he hadn't convinced his older brother. Declan continued to eye him over his glass of beer, amusement clearly reflected in his expression. That was the bad part about having such a large family, Shane thought. Everyone believed they knew you better than you knew yourself.

What was even worse was when they were right.

"Something you care to share with the rest of the

class, brother?" Declan coaxed after taking another long sip of the house beer.

Shane tipped back the half-finished glass of dark ale, then laughed harshly. "It's hard enough sharing a drink with you, let alone a secret—"

Declan grinned triumphantly. "Ah, so you *do* have one. Just as I thought."

He really had to watch how he worded things, Shane warned himself. Most of his immediate family was still tiptoeing around his feelings. Declan was of a mind that his feelings had to be kicked to the curb, his past relationship forgotten about so that he could go on with his life.

And, from the way he was talking, Declan was assuming that it was already a done deal.

"You didn't let me finish—*if* I had a secret to share," he told Declan pointedly.

Shane spared the entrance a quick side glance.

She wasn't going to show.

He had no idea why that bothered him so much or why he kept the fact that he was waiting for someone he'd been forced to interact with today to himself. By keeping quiet about it, he was giving the whole thing far too much importance, much more than it actually deserved or merited.

He supposed it was because he didn't want to seem like a fool in anyone's eyes, least of all a member of his immediate family, which was the way he thought of his father and the seven of them: Tom, Kendra, Bridget, Kari, Logan, Declan and himself.

The others were family—newly found family, at that—and he was still adjusting to the fact, as were some of the others.

Tom and Kari would have embraced anybody who professed to be part of the family, no matter how distant, but he and the rest of them would take varying degrees of time to come around. When he'd first learned the news, he couldn't just stand there, have someone wave a wand over him, declare him to be a Cavanaugh, not a Cavelli, and be instantly okay with that.

Acceptance, as far as he was concerned, took a little more time.

"Well, Pinocchio, as much as I'd like to sit around watching your nose grow, I've got to hit the road." Putting his empty glass on the counter, Declan pulled a five-dollar bill out of his pocket and left it on the counter for the bartender.

"Oh?" Shane moved his stool so that he could get a better look at his brother's face.

"Yeah." There was a rather careless shrug of his shoulders as he elaborated for Shane's benefit. "I've got a date."

"'A date,'" Shane repeated somewhat incredulously.

Declan pretended to look around, as if to pinpoint where the sound was coming from within the center of the din.

"Strange echo in here, Shane. Sounds just like you," Declan said drolly. "Yes, a date," he confirmed.

"You remember dates, don't you, Shane? Things that involve you and a smaller, softer human being." His expression grew more serious. "God, but that witch really did mess you up, didn't she?" Anger momentarily flashed through his green eyes as he thought of the woman who'd broken the engagement and, from the look of it, his brother's heart, as well.

"Don't call her that," Shane said defensively. "It wasn't her fault."

"Well, it sure as hell wasn't yours," Declan said heatedly. "You weren't pretending to be a circus clown and then sprang your secret identity on her. She knew what you were from the start, knew exactly what she was getting into when she agreed to marry you. Aurora's relatively safe when you compare it to other cities of the same population, but things can happen in the best of places.

"To act surprised when they do," he went on, "well, that just means she wasn't the sharpest knife in the drawer, and you're better off without her. I know, I know," he said, raising his hands to fend off Shane's protests, or worse, some kind of defense of the woman he'd come to actively dislike, a defense that for some reason Shane felt honor bound to make. "People say that all the time to someone getting over a breakup, but in this case, I mean it because it really *is* true," Declan insisted.

Declan paused for a moment before leaving. "Why don't you come with me?"

"Like I'd fit right into your date," Shane said, deadpan.

"You would," Declan assured him, warming to his subject. "She's got a sister. From what I hear, a very accommodating sister. Think about it," he coaxed. "She might be just what you need."

There was no way he was up for that. "What I need is to have the rest of this beer and enjoy a little peace and quiet," Shane responded.

Declan looked around at their surroundings. "Well then, you picked the wrong place to go, Shane. No peace and quiet here," he assured his brother.

About to say goodbye, Declan saw his brother's expression change from indifferent to alert. Curious, he turned and saw a petite young redhead wearing an officer's uniform entering the tavern. She was looking around the room, even as her expression seemed to indicate that she wasn't sure why she'd come in the first place.

Glancing back at Shane, Declan realized that his brother had gotten off the bar stool and was now waving to get the pretty redhead's attention.

"On second thought, I see you've already taken care of your needs for the night." He nodded his approval. "My compliments, Shane."

Shane cut him off before Declan could say another word. "Nothing to compliment. We worked on a case together today, and I told her to come share a drink with me if she felt like it."

Declan weighed the merits of the comment his

brother had tendered to the redhead. "Not exactly smooth," he said in critique. "But I guess it's better than nothing. At least it's a start."

"Aren't you going to be late?" Shane prompted, trying to get his brother moving and out the door. "You've got a date, remember?"

"And apparently, so do you," Declan said with a laugh. "See you around, Shane," he promised, taking his leave. "We'll compare notes."

"There'll be no notes to compare," Shane informed his brother tersely.

"So it's like that, is it? Want to keep it all a secret, do you?" It was a rhetorical question, and Declan looked exceedingly pleased. "They're right what they say about still waters." He clapped his brother on the back. "You just keep on paddling, Shane. No matter what, just keep on paddling."

As he made his way to the door, Declan kept one eye on the woman walking toward his brother. Shane was going to be just fine, he thought, pleased about the turn of events. He nodded his approval at the redhead as he passed her.

"Be gentle with him," he said glibly to the woman as he walked by.

Puzzled, Ashley turned to look at the man who'd just made the strange comment, and she frowned to herself. What was *that* all about?

"Did he say something to you?" Shane asked, waiting for Ashley to take a seat at the bar before he sat again himself.

She glanced back at the stranger, but he'd already disappeared through the front door. "Just something about 'being gentle with him.'" She turned back to face Shane. "I'm assuming he was referring to you. Who is he?" she asked, nodding in the direction she'd last seen the stranger.

"Declan," he told her, then added, "one of my misguided brothers." He waved a dismissive hand toward the door Declan had used. "Don't bother paying any attention to him."

"That won't be hard to do since I missed half of what he said," she admitted. Still, the words she *had* heard replayed themselves in her head. Just why did Shane's brother think she was going to do something to hurt the detective?

Shane changed the subject. "Beer okay with you?" he asked. "Or would you like something else?"

She wasn't high maintenance. "Whatever's on tap is fine with me," Ashley answered.

Shane held up his hand to get the bartender's attention. When the man came over, he ordered a beer for Ashley and another one for himself. The order was quickly filled, and then the man made himself scarce.

"I almost went home," Shane admitted after he'd taken a sip of his beer. "I didn't think you were going to show."

She didn't bother telling him that she'd debated before finally coming here. Instead, she told him what had caused the immediate delay. "I had to get

Albert home first. I don't think this place allows dogs on the premises."

"Wait, you took the dog back to the apartment? That's still taped off as a crime scene." At least, he assumed it was. From what he'd picked up from his father, the yellow tape usually remained in place for at least twenty-four hours, if not more.

"No, I took him *home,*" she repeated with emphasis. "My home," she explained when he looked at her as if he was still meandering through a fog.

"Why would you do that?" If anything, the dog should have gone to Aurora's official animal shelter now that they were through processing him.

She would have thought he would have caught on by now. The man obviously had no experience with animals, she decided. "Like I said before, I took him to my house because he was traumatized, because he has to settle down, start trusting people again. And because," she added, her voice softening, "he had just about the saddest eyes I'd ever seen."

Shane laughed, shaking his head. The woman liked to come on tough, but she was a pushover. At least where animals were concerned.

"Doesn't Animal Control have some kind of rule about taking your work home with you?" he asked.

"Albert's not work," she insisted. "If anything, he's a material witness to a murder."

"Right." Shane scrutinized her. Was she being serious? "And what, you expect him to testify?"

"Not directly." She could see that the handsome

detective without a heart thought she'd lost her mind. Since she was here, taking him up on his invitation, she decided she might as well explain her thinking. "If we put the word out that the dog isn't under lock and key, maybe whoever did that to the poor woman will come by to eliminate him. He's a loose end. And that's when I'll arrest him—or her."

He wasn't concerned about the dog. If for some outlandish reason she was right, he was concerned about her. "So in other words, you're setting yourself up to be a target."

That wasn't the way she saw it. "Albert and the boys won't let anything happen to me," she told him with what Shane viewed to be innocent—not to mention misplaced—confidence.

"The boys?" he questioned. Exactly who was staying with her?

"Albert isn't my first pet, or my first dog," she told him. Pausing for a second, she took another quick sip of beer. "I've got a German shepherd and a Labrador at home. I had to make sure they were okay with Albert staying with us for a while before I came to take you up on that warm invitation of yours."

He'd tendered the invitation that way for a reason. She wasn't the type to be pressured into anything, so he'd left the decision up to her.

What she *was,* Shane decided, was the type who seemed to believe that animals were capable of a regular, deep thought process. He, however, didn't.

"And were they?" he asked, humoring her. "Were

they okay with Albert staying with them for a while?"

She knew he was having fun at her expense, but she didn't let on. Instead, she answered him as if he'd asked a serious question.

"They were fine with it after a few rough minutes." When she saw him raise a quizzical brow, she laid it out for him. "You know what I mean. They were checking each other out, sniffing butts and making sure the other dog was okay."

"'Fraid that's a little out of my realm of experience," he told her, still trying to decide whether the soft spot she seemed to have for animals was in her heart or in her head. "I don't smell a fellow detective's butt to make sure he—or she—is on the level."

Ashley laughed at the image he'd created, and he found her laughter to be a soft, enticing sound. Something like what he imagined flowers would sound like if they could make music.

Maybe he should stop at two beers, Shane decided. He just wasn't thinking clearly this afternoon.

"There's nothing that makes me feel safer," she was telling him, taking another sip of the brew the bartender had poured for her, "except for maybe my sidearm. But my sidearm isn't about to go flying across the room to bring down anyone trying to break—or sneak—into my house."

Ashley added the latter mainly for his benefit. She got the impression that he thought of her as some defenseless, fluffy woman instead of a police officer who had police academy training and who was, among other things, rather proficient in martial arts, something she'd learned on her own time.

"A fired bullet can get to its target faster than a dog," Shane pointed out.

She couldn't argue that, but there was another fine point that she *could* argue. "That assumes the person firing can hit what they're firing at."

"And you can't." It was an assumption he'd put together from what she'd just said to him.

She'd done just fine at the firing range—again, on her own time—hitting the target square in the center time and again. But there was a world of difference between a paper target and a person. For one thing, a paper target didn't fire back.

"Never had the occasion to," she admitted. "Guns don't exactly come into play during the course of my day on the job."

He wasn't so sure about that. "How about when you fire a tranquilizer gun?" he asked her.

Still not the same thing. The animal she might be firing at didn't come armed. "They told us to keep firing the rifle until you hit something."

"Not exactly a bumper sticker I'd want on my car," he told her with a laugh. "If you want," he offered, "we can go down to the firing range sometime after your shift is over, and I can give you a few pointers about hitting what you aim at."

She was about to turn him down—it had been all she could do to show up here for that drink. But to not show up would have seemed extremely antisocial. However, she thought better of her refusal of the firing range training.

It wouldn't hurt to pick up a few pointers, Ashley decided. She was always looking to improve herself, and besides, the man was a Cavanaugh. What he might not know, another one of them would. She was looking to move up in the department. It wouldn't hurt her career to be on the right side of a Cavanaugh.

She forced a smile to her lips. "Sounds good," she told him. "We'll have to do it someday."

Shane watched her face as she spoke, wondering if she was serious or just putting him off with the promise of someday. But from what he saw, she was serious.

He nodded. It was settled. "I'll give you a call, then. Set it up."

Ashley took another sip, then let the bitter liquid wind its way down through her throat. Why did people like this stuff? she wondered.

"Find out anything?" she asked. When she saw that her question had caught him off guard, she realized that most likely, although it was an offshoot of her own, albeit silent, thought process, he saw it as coming out of the blue. "About the murderer who kidnapped that baby," she elaborated.

Shane shook his head. God knew it wasn't for his lack of trying.

"Only that the residents of that garden apartment community—the ones who were actually still home when I came to question them—are firm believers in that old adage."

Had she missed something? "*What* old adage?" she asked.

He sighed. "The one that goes, 'See no evil, hear no evil, speak no evil.'"

"If they didn't hear anything—like a woman screaming—that means that either the killer caught her completely by surprise or, more likely, it was someone she knew and she didn't see it coming," Ashley revealed. If there was no screaming, that meant the person had attacked the woman instantly. "And no one saw anything?" she questioned. That meant that the killer was one of those people no one really noticed. A handyman? A mail carrier? That might be one explanation why the victim had opened her door to the killer.

"Not so much as a shadow moving," Shane complained. "Going by the people I did talk to, our victim was killed by an invisible psychopath."

"That wouldn't exactly be something the single women living in that apartment complex would welcome hearing," she commented sympathetically.

Ashley sincerely hoped that Cavanaugh hadn't expressed that sentiment to anyone he'd questioned. The single women who lived in the complex were going to have enough trouble getting any kind of sleep until whoever had done this was caught.

"So I take it that means you're no further along

in the case than you were this morning?" she asked the detective.

Shane wasn't, but he hated the way that sounded, so he rephrased the situation. "I'm waiting on the crime scene investigators to come up with something I can go on."

"In the meantime, did you check out if the rental office has any surveillance cameras pointed anywhere near the crime scene?" she asked. "It seems like these days, every time you turn around, you find yourself staring up into the lens of a surveillance camera. Maybe for once, this invasion of privacy will work in our favor."

She could tell by the look on Shane's face that he hadn't thought of inquiring into that.

"Haven't had the opportunity to check that out yet," he murmured. It was obvious that his omission made him uncomfortable. He *should* have thought of that. "Good point," he allowed. Then, to deflect any further attention to this glaring oversight, he asked her, "Are you thinking of taking the exam for sergeant?"

The idea had crossed her mind, but only in the vaguest sense. "No, why?"

"Well, you seem to have a keener eye for detail than most people in your line of work—"

"My 'line of work' is being a police officer," she pointed out, doing her best not to be insulted by the careless phrase he'd used. "Now, maybe I have ambitions of moving up in the department and maybe

I don't, but either way, that has nothing to do with the way I feel about working in Animal Control. The other officers in the unit and I perform a necessary service," she told him with a touch of pride enveloped in irritation and stamped with swiftly dwindling patience.

It was very obvious to him that she was neither trying to curry favor with him nor impress him, and he had to admit that he liked that. He'd never been all that keen about impressing a superior or the brass, either. He did what he did for his own sake—and the sake of the job itself. He'd never been an out-and-out rebel because it suited his fancy or some preconceived notion he had of himself, but neither was he interested in being a puppet, jumping whenever he was told to jump.

He was beginning to view the officer that fate had caused to cross his path in a whole different light—and with a growing measure of respect, as well as interest.

Chapter 7

They talked a little longer. He noted that she nursed her beer for an uncanny amount of time, despite the fact that he offered to buy her another. He wondered if it was that she didn't really care for beer all that much, or if she didn't want it to seem as if this was a date by any stretch of the imagination and that somehow, allowing him to buy her a second drink qualified as turning this into an official date.

In either case, when she finally did finish the glass of beer she'd been sipping in almost slow motion, he saw Ashley glance at her watch.

"I've got to get on home," she told him. "I don't want to leave the new guy alone in the house for too long."

"Afraid the other two will gang up on him?" he

asked, wondering if that was what was going through her head, or if this was just a convenient excuse that she'd decided to use.

"They wouldn't dare," she told him with a soft laugh he found rather engaging. "For the most part, they're pretty docile and well behaved—unless you happen to be a burglar," she conceded. "But if Albert gets nervous, he might start acting up, and then all bets are off. I'm not sure how the other two will react," she told him as she got off the stool. Smiling, she nodded at the empty glass on the bar. "Thanks for the drink."

She was just saying that to be polite, he thought. "Next time we'll make it something you actually *like* to drink," he couldn't resist saying.

Ashley was about to walk away, but she stopped and stared at him. Why would he say that? "What makes you think I didn't like the beer?"

"At the rate you were going, I'd say that more of it probably evaporated than you managed to actually drink. I don't think I've ever seen anyone drink beer that slowly before. I finally figured out that you hated it, but were too polite to say so."

She surprised him by shaking her head, the corners of her mouth curving in amusement. "Sorry to blow up your theory, but you figured wrong. Beer's definitely not my favorite," she admitted, "but I don't *hate* it." She shrugged, about to divulge a piece of information she generally didn't share with anyone.

"It's a holdover from when I was a kid, a habit I guess I never got over."

"You drank beer as a kid?" he asked, stunned and maybe just a little bit impressed. He would never have been able to get away with something like that in his household. One of his siblings would have immediately told their father what he was doing.

"No, not that." She would have gotten beaten for that in a number of the foster homes she'd lived in. "I just learned to husband everything I got to eat or drink because most of the time, I never knew when I'd be able to get any more."

Just what the hell was she thinking, sharing something like that with this stranger? Just because he seemed nice was *no* reason to let her guard down, even for a minute, Ashley upbraided herself. She couldn't blame it on the alcohol loosening her tongue—she hadn't had enough to drink for that. She supposed seeing that woman today just reminded her of how alone she was, how she hadn't connected to anyone since she'd lost her own baby.

"I'll see you around, Detective," she said, abruptly terminating the decidedly non-Hallmark moment.

"If I find anything out, I'll keep you posted," he promised, raising his voice so that she could hear him. Shane had a feeling that was what she wanted to hear.

Ashley nodded, raising her own voice. "I'd appreciate that."

He watched her leave, allowing himself to likewise appreciate the subtle sway of her hips as she walked away from him, making her way to the front door.

Shane couldn't help wondering if she was even aware of her own femininity and the effect it was having on the men around her.

Banishing the thought, he turned around to face the bar and signaled for the bartender. "What do I owe you for the drinks?"

The bartender took out the receipt pad he carried in the pocket of the green half apron he had tied about his waist. Rather than resorting to a calculator, he did the addition in his head. Everyone knew that Steve favored the old-fashioned way of tallying drinks.

"Didn't go well?" Steve inquired with a touch of sympathy as he gave him the slip of paper.

"I don't really know," Shane admitted honestly. Nor did he know if that bothered him or not. For the time being, he decided to just let it all coast. The case—and the possible kidnapping—was what took front and center for now.

Glancing at the sum, he pulled out two bills and left them on top of the counter. "See you around, Steve."

Shane made it all the way from the tavern to his vehicle before he decided to see if the rental office at the apartment complex was closed yet or if he could find someone still there. He wanted to take a look at any available surveillance tapes from this morning. He prayed that if there were any cameras on the premises, they would be in working order. So many store owners kept broken cameras up for show.

As he drove, Shane berated himself for not thinking of asking about a surveillance camera himself. Granted, he was new on the job, but St. James wasn't even *on* the job and she'd thought of it.

Well, he might not have thought of getting a copy of the recording then, but he had now and that was all that mattered in the long run.

Provided there *was* a recording.

Pulling up to a parking space right in front of the apartment complex's front office, he didn't see the other car at first. There was really nothing about the vehicle to set it apart or to arouse his suspicions as to the owner. It was just a plain white car that had seen better days and could really stand to see the business end of a hose.

It wasn't until he walked into the glass-enclosed, plush rental and leasing office that he realized Ashley had gotten there ahead of him.

Not only that, but the leasing agent, looking rather smitten with her, was handing over a couple of DVDs that he'd obviously just duplicated for her.

"Hope this helps your investigation, Officer," the agent with the baby face and prematurely receding hairline told her.

Ashley graced him with a smile and deftly took

possession of the DVDs. "I do, too," she replied. "Thank you."

"And I'll second that motion," Shane said, adding his voice to the conversation as he walked up behind her.

He thought that coming up like that without any warning would have startled her. Instead the redhead glanced complacently over her shoulder at him and said, "What kept you?"

Instead of surprising her, she had managed to surprise him. "You were expecting me?"

He almost looked boyish with that expression of wonder etched into his features, she thought. "You didn't strike me as being particularly slow, so yes, I figured you'd stop off here to see if you could get a copy of any surveillance tapes before going home."

"What about the dog?" he asked as he watched her leave her signature in exchange for the copies of the surveillance DVDs. She wrote on what appeared to be some sort of ledger. "You said you were anxious to get back to him—or was that just something to throw me off the track?"

"Thank you," she said to the leasing agent, moving the signed ledger closer to him on the desk and picking up the copies of the surveillance DVDs he'd made for her. She tucked the DVDs into the oversize pocket of her jacket. Turning to Shane, she continued with the conversation. "I am. But I didn't see the harm in stopping here to find out if there *was* a surveillance recording." Patting the disks in her pocket, she proclaimed with satisfaction, "Looks like we got lucky."

"What did you see?" he asked as they walked out of the office.

"Nothing yet," she answered, not at all self-consciously. "But at least there *is* something to review."

"And he just made a copy of it for you? Just like that?" Shane asked suspiciously.

She nodded. "The leasing agent was very accommodating. I just asked him for any video surveillance he might have had around that quadrant of the complex. I showed him my badge and told him that I really needed to review the tape at the precinct. I said it had to be from this morning, then I gave him an approximate time frame and crossed my fingers that we'd get lucky."

He noticed that she'd used "we" rather than "I." At least she wasn't a glory hound, he thought, feeling oddly pleased about that.

Masking his reaction, Shane put his hand out for the DVDs. "Let's see if we did," he said to her.

He was not surprised when she made no effort to hand them over to him.

"Tell you what," Ashley proposed. "I'll meet you at the precinct. I'll bring the DVDs, you bring the popcorn and we'll watch them together and find out."

Stopping by his unmarked vehicle, he stared at her. "You're serious."

"Completely," she told him, placing her hand protectively over her pocket. "Remember, possession is nine-tenths of the law," she said glibly.

The petite officer obviously didn't trust him, Shane thought. "I told you that I'd stay in touch if I found something."

"Yes, you did," she acknowledged. "But I happen to know how easy it is to forget to do that," she countered. "You get caught up in watching the tape, get excited if you see something, or *think* you see something, and any promises made to someone not in your department just slip your mind." The scenario was definitely not far-fetched. "I just wanted to make sure you had nothing to berate yourself for," she told him sweetly.

Sliding into the driver's side of her ancient, somewhat dented vehicle, Ashley added a coda to her plan of action.

"I just have to make a pit stop to see if Albert is behaving himself, and if he needs a bathroom break. I'll see you in your squad room at the station in a few minutes," she promised.

If she thought he was falling for that, she was sadly mistaken. "I think I'll just tag along, if you don't mind," he told her.

She saw right through that suggestion. "You don't trust me." She felt she knew the answer to that. It wasn't even a question, really. It was more of an assumption.

He had a counter answer to that. "Let's just say

I'm coming along to make sure that the chain of evidence isn't compromised."

She stared at him. Did he think she was going to tamper with something on the surveillance recording? "Exactly what is that supposed to mean?"

He thought quickly and came up with a plausible explanation for what he'd just said that wouldn't put her nose out of joint. "That everyone isn't as trusting as I am, and it's actually better for you if I do tag along so I can tell anyone who thinks otherwise that the evidence didn't stray or get altered in any manner, shape or fashion. Think of me as a witness to your basic integrity."

She didn't really believe him. But she only fought battles she felt she had a chance of winning. Ashley had a feeling this detective could go on like this for the rest of the afternoon and half the night.

So, instead of arguing, she just shrugged and told him, "Suit yourself."

Shane fully intended to, although he did refrain from saying, "I usually do."

He followed her in his car.

The residential community Ashley pulled into was, according to his vague recollection of something his father had once said, the oldest one in Aurora. The seven hundred and fifty homes within the development were built up around an initial cluster of two-story family homes.

Even so, although the homes were all verging on

being approximately forty years old, he saw none that even remotely appeared to be in disrepair. There were a number, though, that looked as if they could stand to have a little remodeling done or, at the very least, refreshed just a bit.

He even saw several houses that still had the old-style shake roofs on them rather than the far safer clay tiles that most homeowners had gravitated toward in the past twenty or so years.

Currently there was a "Take pride in your classic home" movement going on in Aurora. And that was only to the good, he imagined.

The house she pulled up in front of looked as if it was in need of a fresh coat of paint, but the roof was new and there was a flower garden out front that appeared to have recently been the recipient of a good deal of loving care.

"Nice house," he said after he parked his car beside hers in the driveway and got out.

"Thanks. It was all I could afford," she said offhandedly.

The house had been sold as a fixer-upper, and any spare time she'd had in the past two years had gone into working on it. Though it might not look it, the house had come a long way. When she'd bought it, the walls had been removed. The former owner had died here, and no one had missed the old man until three weeks later. By then, the smell had gotten into the very walls as well as the rugs. Removal was the only way to get rid of it.

"I'm working on it bit by bit," she told him.

"This isn't your parents' home?" He'd just assumed, given the home's age, as well as its size, that she'd inherited it from her parents, one or both of whom he assumed might still be living on the premises.

Ashley wasn't about to tell him how the house represented a lot of scrimping and saving on her part—she'd even held down two jobs at one point. Every penny had gone into its down payment. As a child, she'd always dreamed of having a house to come home to for something longer than just three or four months at a stretch.

And now she did.

"Why would you assume that?" she challenged, wanting to know.

Had he said something wrong? A lot of people inherited their parents' home. Nonetheless, given her tone, he decided to tread lightly here.

"I just thought that, given the age of the development, you got this from your parents."

"I bought this house," she proclaimed tersely. "Put every dime I had at the time into it. Nobody gave me anything. Ever." Then, adopting a slightly milder tone, she changed the subject. "Are they assigning anyone else to this case?"

"Why?" he asked warily.

She answered him honestly. He might be a detective, but she had a gut feeling he wasn't *that* kind of a detective. "Because so far, you don't exactly strike me as a hot-shot detective, Cavanaugh. I'm thinking maybe Homicide isn't your thing."

His eyes narrowed. "I'm working on it," he told her evenly.

She took a breath, telling herself that to insult this man wasn't going to be productive. He was, after all, a Cavanaugh.

Ashley willed herself to calm down. "Sorry, I guess that came off a little combative. I didn't mean to sound as if I was spoiling for a fight. Certain things just set me off," she admitted.

"I take it you're not on good terms with your parents," he concluded.

He himself couldn't really imagine what that was like. But then, his parents had been unbelievably understanding, even during those couple of years when he'd thought he'd known everything and they'd known absolutely nothing. They'd waited him out until he'd realized that he was the reigning authority on very little.

"Not particularly," she answered, hoping that would shut him down. Taking out her house key, she inserted it into the lock.

"Sorry to hear that."

He sounded as if he meant that. It made her feel guiltier about her sudden flare of temper. So much so that she added, "Maybe I would be if they were still around, but they died when I was four—or so I was told."

Actually, the qualifying phrase was a lie. Not that

she hadn't been told. One of the dozens of social services women who had traipsed through her life had told her that she'd been found near the burning car. But that woman had had a bad temper and the emotional range of a lemon, so as soon as she could, Ashley had researched the incident for herself.

She had wound up going through every single news story about a car accident taking two lives and leaving a toddler as the only survivor. It had taken her more than six months, but she'd finally come across a couple of lines in one paper, a few more in another. Working her way backward, she'd greedily absorbed every detail she could find. Even so, there hadn't been all that much.

She never had uncovered a name. Or the cause of the accident.

Shane looked at her, not knowing what to say, only aware that he should say *something.* "Saying I'm really sorry sounds pretty trite, given the situation," he finally confessed.

She shrugged off his words. "Hey, it happened a long time ago, and until this morning, you and I didn't even know each other so there's no reason for you to be sorry about *any* of it." Ashley lifted her chin proudly. She refused to be on the receiving end of pity, no matter how well intentioned. She wasn't that homeless waif to be pitied anymore.

To prevent the detective from saying anything more and making them both uncomfortable, Ashley turned the key quickly and pushed open the door.

Even before she entered the house, she heard the new dog barking up a storm. The other two dogs, bless 'em, had remembered their training. Whether it was instinct or a keen sense of smell that helped them tell her apart from anyone else, they knew it was her unlocking the door. Because of that, there was no reason for either of them to bark.

The moment she walked in, the two older dogs surrounded her, vying for her attention, each wanting to be the first one to be petted.

"Hey, hey, hey, guys, it's only been a little more than an hour. You couldn't have missed me that much." She laughed. "Has the new guy been giving you trouble?" she quipped, amused at the abundant show of affection.

Looking down at the terrier, who was growling at Cavanaugh, daring him to take a step closer, Ashley bent to pick up the dog.

"What did I tell you about your attitude, Albert?" she chided. "You've got to make an effort to get along with the guys." She shifted the dog so that his small face was looking up directly at hers. "You're safe here and there's nothing to worry about, but you can't give everyone a hard time, understand?"

In response, instead of barking, the dog licked her face.

"No, that's not going to get you off the hook," she told him, laughing again.

Despite her protest, Shane could see that the display of affection got to her.

She seemed completely at ease, as well as almost like a completely different person around the dogs. It was then that he realized what was different about her. Her guard wasn't up, and she wasn't radiating tension the way she seemed to earlier, when she was just around people.

It hadn't been a fluke back at the apartment complex. Animals apparently responded to her, and she responded to them.

"You make it sound as if they understand you," he observed.

"Of course they do." The look on her face indicated that she didn't understand why he would doubt that even for a moment.

Chapter 8

"You're not actually planning on keeping that dog, are you?" Shane asked once they had arrived back at the precinct.

True to her promise, she'd only spent a few minutes at her house. Once she was sure that the terrier hadn't gotten into anything that he shouldn't, that he hadn't decided to use the inside of the house as his own personal bathroom and that the other two dogs hadn't ganged up on him in her absence, she had closed up the house and driven back to the police station.

Rather than follow in the detective's wake, something, most likely her ever-present sense of competition, had urged her to take the lead. She made certain to keep his car in her rearview mirror at all times.

She also made certain to stay ahead of him for the duration. If he sped up, so did she.

Hurrying up the front stairs to the entrance now, Ashley glanced in the detective's direction. Why would he ask that, and why would he even want to know?

"Why?" she asked bluntly. "Do you want him?"

"Me? No." He had nothing against dogs, but then, on the other hand, he didn't really have anything *for* them, either. "I just thought that since you already have two large dogs, that particular one would be too much work for you to take on. He seemed a little hyper to me," he added when Ashley didn't answer him at first.

When she did answer, her voice was crisp and cool, with an added element that he couldn't quite identify. "Jack Russell terriers aren't exactly known for being calm and laid-back. And this one has had more than his share of drama and trauma. That being said, everyone deserves to be loved."

Her answer gave him pause. Shane looked at her as he held open the heavy glass door. He got the definite impression that she wasn't talking just about the dog anymore. If he didn't know better, he would have said that she identified with the now homeless animal.

It sounded rather strange, not to mention possibly far-fetched, but Shane couldn't really shake the feeling that he was right, now that he'd put it into words for himself.

Did she identify with homeless, unloved creatures? He found himself more than a little curious about this pushy, headstrong officer. Looking at her, he wouldn't have thought she was unloved at all. Quite the opposite. But then, although he had no such problem himself, he'd come to recognize that self-image had little to nothing to do with what a person saw reflected in their mirror in the morning.

"After you lost your parents, did any of your relatives step up?" He saw a dark look enter Ashley's eyes, a look that warned him to back off now if he knew what was good for him. But he was already in this and saw no other way but to go on with his question, to stick with the subject until he got an answer. "You know, did anyone offer to take you in?" he persisted when Ashley said nothing.

Her voice was a little strained when she finally did answer his question.

Strained and distant.

"They couldn't determine who my parents were. The interior of the car had burned to a crisp, as had the two people in it. No identification of any kind was ever found. The way I saw it," she said with a careless shrug, "if there was no identification, no one was forced to come forward and claim me."

What a strange way to put it, he thought, as if she believed that if anyone was related to her, they'd clung gratefully to the cloak of anonymity and deliberately stayed silent.

He knew he should just shut up, but he couldn't

seem to help himself. He supposed this was proof that he really was a Cavanaugh, if he ever needed it. Cavanaughs had a tendency to pursue such things as family and honor beyond all reasonable boundaries.

"Were you ever adopted?" he asked gently.

Her expression was close to stony as she raised her chin almost defiantly, as if daring him to make something of it. "No, I was never adopted. I wasn't cute enough, I suppose," she told him tersely. "I went the other route. Foster homes, some good, some not so much. I was sent back a lot because I wasn't respectful enough." She sounded proud of the fact.

Her mouth curved almost sardonically as Ashley recalled the foster parent who had made that criticism about her.

"In one case, that meant that I wouldn't allow my foster father to use me as his substitute wife when his real one went out of town to visit her sister."

Shane felt the very air leave his lungs as the horror of that situation hit him. Things like that had never even remotely touched his own childhood or the childhood of anyone he'd grown up with. It wasn't until he'd become a cop that he was even aware that there were children who lived with that sort of a threat every night of their lives until they were old enough to either run away or exact their revenge.

"Did he…?" He purposely left the words unspoken, giving her the option of filling in her own version if she chose to.

Ashley raised her eyes to his. "He tried," she answered. "Just once he tried. I grabbed the closest weapon—his cherished baseball bat—and took a swing at a place I wasn't about to let him use. I got sent back the next morning." Although the man had been livid, he hadn't filed any charges against her, hadn't exacted any punishment. He'd been in the wrong and had obviously sensed that she wasn't afraid to give her version of the events. He'd chosen silence as the best option and had her sent back to the group home.

Shane found himself vacillating between anger and feeling sorry for her. "How old were you?"

"Ten." The single word had an edge to it, as if she was waiting for him to challenge her.

Shane began to understand why she was closer to animals than to people. From the sound of it, she had never found anyone she could trust, or relate to.

"You know," he told her as the elevator arrived, "I can take it from here if you're tired and want to get back to your house. It is getting late," he pointed out.

"That's okay, I'll just tag along," she said with a touch of sarcasm, getting on the elevator. "That is, if you don't mind a glorified dog catcher hanging around you while you examine the evidence," she told him, deliberately making reference to the label he'd affixed to her position.

Being exposed to her a little more than he had been earlier, the phrase he'd used before was now a source of embarrassment to him.

"I didn't mean any disrespect…" he began.

"Yeah, of course you did," she contradicted mildly. "But don't worry about it," Ashley told him in the next breath, dismissing the incident. "It wasn't exactly the first time someone thought what I do is inconsequential and it sure as hell isn't going to be the last time."

"Is that why you're looking to get out of the section and into Homicide?" It seemed like a clear-cut choice to him.

It would have been simpler just to say yes, but Ashley had never been one for taking the simple, expedient route.

"It's more a matter of getting to use my brain a little more. I like being challenged, like having to use my brain to figure out what happened, how all the pieces fit together even if they don't seem to at first. I really don't see all that much of that sort of thing working with Animal Control." She laughed softly to herself. "There, it's more of a catch-and-release type of situation."

"Except that you don't do much releasing," Shane interjected. It was more of a guess on his part, given the facts he'd just picked up today.

Rather than butt heads over the point, she referred to the obvious. "If that was true, my place would look like a zoo," she pointed out. The elevator bell dinged, and the doors yawned open. She looked at him. "Your floor?"

"This is it," he confirmed, gesturing for her to get out first.

Bypassing the squad room, he led her to what amounted to a small alcove with a door located further down the hall. The alcove was in the complete opposite direction.

Opening the door, he allowed her to look in first. The room was slightly larger than it originally appeared, which still gave it the dimensions of a large walk-in closet. There were a total of three monitors lined up next to one another with three desks beneath them, all with keyboards and DVD players.

"Pick a seat," he said, gesturing in the general area of the desks. She picked a chair on the left. Rather than take the one on the other end, he chose the one in the middle, sitting next to her. "Since it looked as if there were several surveillance recordings and you wanted to come along, I thought we could split the work between us, get it done in half the time."

"Your lieutenant won't mind my viewing these?" Ordinarily she would have gone right at it, but since he was being nice, she thought it was only fair not to let him get into trouble because he was letting her join the investigation, at least unofficially.

"Captain," he declared. "He's a captain, not a lieutenant. And all he cares about is how many cases are cleared. We're down a few people, not to mention my partner who's on extended medical leave, recovering from that gunshot wound." It seemed to him that they were *always* down a few people. "I figure the captain would welcome an extra set of eyes."

"Once you tell him," Ashley ventured, waiting for him to comply.

"Yeah, once I tell him," he agreed, making absolutely no effort to turn that hypothetical situation into reality. For one thing, the captain had gone home for the day.

"Okay, let's get started," he suggested, then looked at her. "You've got the recordings," he reminded her.

Ashley was already retrieving the disks from her pocket. She placed all four of them next to one another on the desk.

"Take your pick," she told him, gesturing at the disks. He took the two closest to him, and she moved the other two closer to her.

"Too bad I forgot to bring the popcorn," he commented drolly.

"Next time," she said automatically.

She was being flippant, but he rather liked the idea of that, of working with her again at some other, future date.

"'Next time,'" Shane echoed. "Okay, here goes nothing," he said as he inserted the first of his disks into his machine.

She had already done the same with hers. An image flickered on the screen and she found herself watching the film taken from one corner of the complex.

The recordings featured the area where the victim's apartment was located. They found themselves watching an exodus of various vehicles from the parking lot as a number of the residents drove off for work this morning. The influx of a few cars coming *into* the complex and its parking lots represented either friends dropping by, or others swinging by to pick up people as presumably part of a carpool run.

In a couple of cases, the cars belonged to the complex's maintenance men arriving for work.

Watching the endless monotony broken up by the occasional vehicle or resident walking by with either mail to send off, utilizing the mail slot in a nearby bank of mailboxes, or trash to throw into the local Dumpster, Ashley began to feel her eyelids getting seriously heavy. Any second now, she thought she was going to drop off to sleep.

"Gives new meaning to the word *boring*, doesn't it?" she heard Cavanaugh commenting.

Her eyes flew open. Ashley couldn't help wondering if he'd just watched her falling asleep and was having fun at her expense.

Taking in a subtle breath to pull herself together and desperately try to come to, Ashley murmured flippantly, "We should make a copy of this and sell it as a cure for insomnia."

And that was when she saw it. Saw someone walking up to the apartment door she recognized as the victim's.

Gripping the armrests, Ashley straightened. She was instantly wide awake and alert. "Hold on, I think this is it. I think this recording caught whoever went into the victim's apartment this morning."

His sense of observation sharpened to a fine point, Shane moved his chair closer to hers, craning his neck to see.

"Can you make out the face?" he asked with a touch of eagerness.

"I'm not sure I can even make out the person's back," she confessed, frustrated. The quality of the recording was exceedingly poor. The tape had obviously been used over and over again to make recordings. "Is that a stocky man or a plus-size woman?"

Shane's shoulders rose and fell in a silent admission that told her he had no clue.

"You got me," he admitted. "I can send this down to the lab wizard, see if she can make it any clearer for us."

"'Lab wizard'?" she repeated quizzically.

But Shane was quite serious. He nodded to her silent query. "Brenda." Since the name obviously meant nothing to her, he gave her a more extensive introduction. "She's the chief of detectives' daughter-in-law," he added as a sidebar.

"Of course she is."

Ashley shook her head, astounded, although she tried not to appear that way. What was it like, she couldn't help wondering, having a family who always had your back, who always looked out for you, no matter what? Who seemed to have more members than a small Third World nation? She would have given *anything* to have grown up knowing the answer to that question.

"Tell me, is there an area of this police department that doesn't have a Cavanaugh in it?" They probably even had someone in the maintenance department, working undercover, she mused.

"Animal Control comes to mind," Shane quipped, then he suddenly recalled, "although the vet who treats the dogs in the K-9 unit is the chief's niece."

In truth, Shane was just getting the lay of the land himself since, prior to being on the receiving end of the somewhat shocking news bulletin that he and his family were actually Cavanaughs, he hadn't really paid all that much attention to the fact that there was a rather large number of Cavanaughs spread throughout the entire police department.

"Somehow," Ashley was saying, referring to the fact that Patience Cavanaugh Coltrane was the K-9 Unit's go-to vet, "I kind of figured there had to be."

The thought of a family that large was almost too hard for her to fathom. There'd always only been her. Even the few kids in the system she'd allowed herself to get close to over the years wound up fading away for one reason or another.

And none quicker than Joel.

"Well, I guess you might as well put your relatives to use," Ashley responded. "Maybe Brenda can clean up the disk so we can at least make out the visitor's gender."

Even as she said it, Ashley wasn't quite ready

to give up the recording just yet. Instead, she fast-forwarded it, hoping that perhaps they'd wind up getting a better look at the person once he or she left the apartment again.

But although she went through a sufficient amount of the recording, no one stepped out of the apartment. Instead, she fast-forwarded the recording to the point where she saw herself approaching the apartment window.

And as she watched, she saw herself removing the screen and window pane.

Shane blew out a breath, frustrated as well as mystified. Where was the perpetrator? "Well, we have a decent recording of you breaking into the apartment," he commented.

She ignored the flippant observation. "Where did the perp go?" She wanted to know.

"There was no one in the apartment when you got in?" he asked.

She took offense to that. "Don't you think I would have said something if there'd been anyone in there when I looked through the window to see that woman lying there?" she demanded.

In contrast to her heated question, Shane merely remained silent, waiting for the answer to the question he'd asked.

Ashley sighed, relenting. "Just the victim," she said. Despite her bravado, it was easy to see that she was clearly stunned. She looked at Shane. "All I can think of is that the person must've gone out through the patio when he or she heard me crawling through the window. Gone through it and taken the baby along with them."

"Well, CSI went over the whole apartment. If there was anything outside on the patio—not to mention any*one*—they would have found it," he told her.

The people in the unit were only human, right? "If they knew to look there. Maybe there was something they overlooked," Ashley proposed.

Shane saw the eager look in her eyes, and he could almost hear what she was thinking. "You want to go back there."

Leaning back in the chair, she spread her hands wide. "I don't think we have a choice. The killer seemed to know that he could get away that way—if it was a he," Ashley qualified. Leaning forward again, she stared at the frozen form on the monitor. No matter how long she looked, she couldn't make out the gender of the figure.

Shane looked at the monitor thoughtfully. "I think we did establish one thing, though."

What had she missed? It goaded her that he'd picked up on something that she obviously had overlooked. "What? What did we establish?" she asked, mystified. "We don't even know if it was a man or a woman."

"Granted," he said, inclining his head to give her that point. "But whoever it was, the victim apparently knew them."

"What makes you say that?" She'd thought the

same thing, but wanted to hear his reasoning. It would validate and give substance to her own interpretation.

"Easy. There wasn't even a slight hesitation when the victim opened the apartment door. She let the caller right in." Shane rose from the desk where he'd done his viewing. "It's late," he declared. "Let's drop that recording off at the lab. Then in the morning, we can either watch Brenda work her magic, or go back to the victim's apartment and have a closer look around that patio."

It sounded like a plan to her. She was all for going over the apartment a second time—or in her case, a first time. "Maybe we could also talk to some of the neighbors, see if they saw or heard anything," she suggested, doing her best not to sound as if she was a novice at this.

"Already did that," he told her.

She pushed back the wave of disappointment when it occurred to her that his investigation had to be, perforce, incomplete.

"But there were a lot of them who'd gone off to work by the time you did your canvas. Maybe one of them left just as the perp was coming in. Could be that one of them saw something, remembered something." She looked at him. "It's worth a shot," she proposed.

"Considering we're currently firing blanks, sure, why not?" he answered gamely.

Most likely, they were just spinning their wheels,

but there was a small chance that the feisty little animal control officer could be right, he thought.

Shane popped the DVD he wanted Brenda to look at out of the machine and slipped it into an evidence envelope. He then placed the other three disks together in an envelope he also marked as evidence.

"Okay, let's register this with the lab tech so that Brenda sees it first thing in the morning," Shane told her.

"Sounds good to me," she told him, shutting off her machine before she left the room.

The thought briefly occurred to Ashley that he was treating her as if she was part of a team. The corners of her mouth curved as she allowed herself to savor the notion just for a moment or two.

After all, what did it hurt?

Chapter 9

They were back at it bright and early the next morning. It didn't surprise Shane to find Ashley waiting for him by his desk a few minutes before the start of his shift. Hers, too, Shane imagined. It made him wonder if she had a life outside the department.

He could identify with that.

They lost no time in going to see Brenda down in the lab.

"Brenda, this is Ashley St. James. She's attached to Animal Control. Ashley, this Brenda Cavanaugh, Dax's wife and the chief of detectives' daughter-in-law—as well as a legend in her own right," Shane said, making the initial introductions between the two women.

He'd brought Ashley down to the basement where

the crime scene investigation unit, as well as the computer tech unit, was tucked away. The latter was very nearly the solo domain of the vibrant young woman he'd just introduced her to.

Accustomed to the outpouring of charm whenever one of the Cavanaugh men found themselves in need of her unique skills, Brenda was not taken in by the complimentary words. Instead she pretended to look at the detective suspiciously.

"Just how many hours of sleep is this going to cost me, Shane? You're laying the glowing adjectives on with a shovel."

Shane grinned, looking, Ashley caught herself thinking, almost boyish. He certainly looked a great deal friendlier than he had when he'd first come on the scene yesterday morning.

"I'm just giving you your due, Brenda," he told the computer tech. "I'm just giving you your due."

Brenda refrained from laughing out loud. In truth, she didn't mind this game they all played with her. She had a skill, and she enjoyed using it to aid the police department, not to mention the vastly sprawling family she'd married into.

"Part of my 'due,'" she informed Shane, "is that I wasn't born yesterday—or the day before."

"And yet, there you are, looking hardly older than a teenager while being cleverer than the lot of us put together." He turned toward Ashley. "If it can be done with a computer," he told her with a touch of family pride, "Brenda will do it."

"Shane." There was a warning note in Brenda's tone. She pushed her chair back from her desk to study him for a moment. "This is getting to sound worse and worse. Just what sort of a miracle are you asking for?"

Shane sighed for effect, then leveled with her. "I need a face, Brenda."

This time she did laugh. Of all the things he could complain about, this was not one of them. In her humble opinion, the Cavanaughs had cornered the market in good looks.

"Trust me," she told him, "the one you have is more than just presentable."

He held the disk up to focus her attention. "And the one on here could lead us to a killer."

"That's more like it." Interest had instantly entered Brenda's eyes. There was nothing she loved more than a challenge to her inherent abilities. She shook her head. "You really do know how to push all the right buttons in my case, don't you, Shane?"

"Your husband's a cop and a crack shot," Shane replied innocently. "I wouldn't dare press any of your buttons."

Delight was evident in her voice. "You, Shane Cavanaugh, would dare anything." Her eyes shifted over to Ashley. "This one had the word *trouble* stamped on his forehead when he was three minutes old. I would watch my step if I were you."

"There's nothing to watch," Ashley replied politely. "The detective and I are only working together temporarily."

Brenda studied the younger woman for a moment. She did *not* look convinced. Instead what she looked was amused. "That's what they all say," she assured Ashley with a wide smile.

"They?" What was the tech talking about? "Who's 'they'?" Ashley was curious in spite of herself.

"Every Cavanaugh wife who started out thinking she was immune to the Cavanaugh male charm," Brenda informed her matter-of-factly.

Well, whatever trance the other women had obviously fallen under, that was *not* about to happen to her.

"First time for everything," Ashley told her, dead certain that she was not about to "fall victim" to anything that had a legend built around it. She thought for herself and danced to her own piper. Detective Shane Cavanaugh was a good-looking man, but that played absolutely no part in anything, she thought stubbornly. "We got an image on the surveillance disk of the person we think killed our victim. Can you enhance the figure enough for us to at least determine if it's a man or a woman?"

Brenda looked quizzically at the disk that Shane handed her, her brow furrowing slightly. "What's on here, anyway? Private photographs of the Invisible Man?"

"Or the Invisible Woman," Shane supplied. Personally, what he'd seen had struck him as being too gruesome for something a woman would have done, but he knew that there were a lot of people who would disagree with him. Women were not really the gentler sex; they were actually the tougher one.

Brenda looked at the disk for a moment, then shook her head. She had a feeling she had her work cut out for her. "You two certainly don't ask for much, do you?"

"If we didn't," Shane pointed out, "we wouldn't be coming to you, Oh Mighty and Powerful Wizard, now, would we? A middle-of-the-road techie would have been more than sufficient in that case."

Brenda laughed to herself. "You do know how to pour it on, I'll give you that." She didn't believe half of what he was saying to her, but she would have been lying if she didn't admit that she liked hearing it. She glanced toward the woman Shane had brought with him. "Like I said—and it bears repeating," she assured Ashley, "I'd be careful around this one if I were you. *Very* careful."

If you couldn't fight 'em, join 'em, Ashley thought philosophically. If being knocked around between foster homes had taught her anything, it was how to be flexible, to roll with the punches and say anything that allowed you to walk away from a bad situation in one piece whenever possible.

That wasn't the case here, but she didn't want to do or say anything to get on the tech expert's bad side. So she agreed with her.

"I'll be sure to keep that in mind," Ashley replied

in a voice that clearly announced she really wasn't worried about being disoriented by the handsome, dark-haired detective.

"What can you tell me about the DVD?" Shane coaxed Brenda, even though she had only popped it into her machine.

Brenda looked up at him thoughtfully from where she was seated at her desk. "Well, right off the bat I can tell you one main thing."

That wasn't possible, Ashley thought. The woman *had* to be pulling their legs. She hadn't even called up the first frame yet. But, seeing as how this computer tech was the chief of D's daughter-in-law, she held up her end of the conversation.

"And that would be?" Ashley asked.

Brenda managed to maintain a straight face. "A watched computer tech never boils."

This time a small, amused smile escaped and curved Ashley's mouth. At least the chief of D's daughter-in-law had a sense of humor, she thought.

"Nice to know."

"You didn't tell me you were auditioning for the comedy club," Shane said wryly to Brenda.

The look on Brenda's face was pure innocence. "You never asked me."

"Anything else you'd like to get out of your system?" he prompted.

"Nope, that about does it," Brenda replied. She was already dealing with the grainy features of the recording. "Come back later," she suggested. "I'll see if I have anything for you."

Shane glanced in Ashley's direction before saying, "Good enough for me."

"Now we canvas the apartment complex?" Ashley asked as they left the lab and walked down the hall to the elevator.

"Unless you have a better idea."

In actuality, Shane was entertaining a better idea of his own, but it really had nothing to do with the case they were dealing with. Besides, at this point, he thought it might be a smarter move if he played it safe and went about plotting his campaign to win over the sharp-eyed officer slowly. If he did that, he could build up his momentum and she couldn't really accuse him of being shallow.

"No, no better idea," she replied. "As a matter of fact, canvassing the apartment complex sounds pretty good to me," she told him. "You never know what you might come up with the second time around."

Funny, he thought. That was something his father had said to him during the pep talk he'd given him after Kitty had broken off their engagement.

"You can't just shut yourself off from life, Shane. You have to pick yourself up and get back into the game in order to heal. You never know what you might come up with the second time around. Look at me—I never thought I'd ever fall in love with another woman after all those good years I had with your mother. I was a one-woman man whose one woman had passed away. I thought that was it for me—but obviously I thought wrong. You are, too," his father had assured him.

At the time he'd thought it was just empty talk. But maybe not, he caught himself musing as he stood beside Ashley.

The elevator announced its arrival with a muted ding.

"So," Shane began as he followed her into the elevator. The doors closed rhythmically and took them to the first floor. "*Are* you leaning toward Homicide?"

She looked at him. Why was he asking that? Was it a trick question? Cavanaugh couldn't possibly entertain the idea that the victim had just suddenly expired. Of course it was a homicide.

"Well, it's obvious that someone butchered her to get her baby, isn't it?" she asked, indicating that she was a hundred percent behind the idea that this couldn't be anything else *but* a homicide.

He laughed and shook his head. She'd misunderstood. "No, I mean for your choice of a department. Is Homicide where you want to work?"

"Oh." They'd touched on this last night, but she supposed she hadn't been very clear about it. Being vague had been a way of life for her for a long time. Growing up, she'd found it safer not to take a definite stand on anything unless she had no other choice or option open to her.

The elevator arrived on the first floor, its doors yawning open and allowing them to disembark.

"Yes," she replied a little formally. "I've decided that Homicide is my first choice," she replied, answering his question.

He didn't see it as an obvious choice for someone like her, even though his sisters had gravitated toward that department. His sisters, Bridget, Kendra and Kari, *never* took the obvious path when it came to anything.

"Why?" he asked her. "Why Homicide instead of, say, Burglary or Narcotics?"

That was simple enough for her to answer. "Because death is the ultimate insult, and somebody has to speak for the dead."

"So, you speak for the dead as well as for the animals." He allowed that to simmer in his brain for a minute. "Tell me," he asked, "where does the average *breathing* person come into all this?"

That, too, had an easy answer. "Beneath my radar," she informed him glibly.

For a moment he thought she was kidding. But one look into her eyes negated that impression. "You're serious," he realized.

"As serious as a third strike for a career criminal," she told him without blinking an eye.

He could see, given her upbringing, why she might feel that way about it. However, he was just as convinced that she shouldn't continue on in this vein. This wasn't a life, it was a by-the-numbers existence, he judged, and as such it meant that she was getting very little out of life by way of enjoyment, at least in his opinion.

Shane figured that really had to change if, just possibly, Ashley had a chance of changing, too.

Whoa, he warned himself. He'd only known her for a little more than a day. That amount of time didn't make him an expert on anything, much less an apparently emotionally wounded young woman.

"Why don't we go in my car?" he suggested when he saw that she was heading toward her own vehicle.

Ashley stopped, glancing over toward the vehicle she drove every day, the Animal Control van.

"Why?" she asked.

"Because in these hard times, it wouldn't be a bad thing to save on gas and use one car." He could almost see what she was thinking. "And if we drove up to the complex in yours, people might not take us seriously."

Ashley fixed him with a look. "The dog catcher thing again," she quipped.

He wanted to spare her feelings. After all, she performed a necessary service. But by the same token, people would regard her as a lightweight, not a real officer. She needed to look the part from head to foot and, by association, that applied to her vehicle, as well.

"Right on the first guess," he told her.

Ashley stood where she was for a moment, seriously debating continuing on her way to her van. It would have been her act of defiance.

But in the end, she conceded that Cavanaugh did have a point. People didn't take people working for Animal Control as seriously as they took regular officers. And she did very much want to be taken seriously.

Who knew? This might be her only shot at showing what she knew and what she was capable of. She didn't want to blow it because she favored her own vehicle over his.

"Okay." Ashley gave in. "We'll take your car."

He refrained from making any sort of acknowledging comment, thinking that it might backfire on him and turn her off just when he'd made up his mind to find out what it took to open this complicated woman up, not shut her down.

The drive over to Monica Phillips's apartment complex was quick this time of the morning. Once there, they began by knocking on the door of the victim's nearest neighbor.

A middle-aged woman answered on the third knock. Standing in the doorway, holding the door to partially shield herself, the woman looked the pair over critically as well as impatiently. The TV could be heard in the background, and she appeared to be eager to return to her program.

"Whatever you're peddling, I already bought it," she snapped as she began to close the door again.

Shane stuck his hand on the door, catching it before it had a chance to meet the doorframe. He was obviously a lot stronger than the woman, even though they appeared evenly matched when it came to weight. But he did have close to a foot on her.

"How about questions?" he asked her.

The woman blinked, staring contemptuously at him. "What?"

"We're peddling questions," Shane repeated. "How would you like to answer some for us?" he persisted.

It was obvious that her answer was no. "Look, I'm busy and I don't have any time for games—"

This time, as she tried to slam the door, she was prevented not just by the strength of Shane's hand, but by the shield and ID he held up in front of her.

The sight of both—as well as a second set that Ashley held up—caught the victim's neighbor off guard. For approximately fifteen seconds. And then she sneered. "You think I don't know you can get those in every back alley in this town?"

"Actually, you can't," Shane contradicted. There'd been a campaign to eliminate fake police IDs, and it had been successful. "We just need you to answer a few questions about your neighbor, Monica Phillips."

The look of suspicion on the woman's wrinkled face grew. As did, surprisingly enough, a tone that could only be described as protective. "You trying to pin something on Monica?"

"Why?" Ashley spoke up, snagging the woman's attention. "What have you heard?"

"I ain't heard nothin'," the woman stated. "That poor kid's got enough to deal with. That no-good boyfriend of hers took off over a month ago, yelling that she was on her own. That the baby she was carrying wasn't his. All that worthless piece of garbage ever did was get into fights with her. Knocked her around a bit, too, although she never said as much. But you can't fool me," she bragged. "I saw the bruises.

"One of the neighbors even called in a cop on them when they got into a really bad one," she volunteered, contemptuous of the act of being an informant, "but not me. Not me," she repeated as if saying it twice drove the point home that much more clearly. "You ask me, she's better off without him."

In a way, the story was all too familiar, Shane thought. "Not anymore," he said dryly.

The comment had the woman in the doorway frowning. She looked from the detective to the officer with him. "Why? They get back together?" she asked, her curiosity piqued.

"No, she's dead," he replied flatly, watching the woman's expression.

Her eyes instantly became so huge, they looked as if they were in danger of falling out and rolling away. "Who killed her?" she demanded angrily.

"That's what we're trying to find out," Ashley said before Shane had the opportunity.

"It was that rotten boyfriend, wasn't it?" the woman demanded. Then, before either of them had a chance to answer her, she became more emphatic. "It was. It was him, I just know it. The minute he took off, she should have done the same—in the opposite direction."

"Do you think you could describe him to a sketch artist for us?" Shane asked. "It won't take long," he promised.

The woman glanced at her watch. "I've got a… friend coming over in an hour," she said. "Maybe tomorrow."

In his experience, tomorrow wasn't something that automatically arrived on the heels of today. Half the time, it got all turned around and disappeared. "I think that it might be in everyone's best interest if you came to the precinct with us—"

But Ashley interrupted. "I can do a sketch here if you prefer," she told the woman.

Surprise registered on Shane's face as he looked at her. "You sketch?" he asked incredulously.

Ashley shrugged. It was something that came so naturally to her, she didn't even think about it. It was just part of who she was. Capturing her surroundings on paper as a kid had given her solace, a sense of unity that she'd needed.

"Decently enough to be able to tell the sketches apart," she answered.

"In other words, they don't all come out looking like sickly stick figures?" he offered.

"Not that I know of," Ashley answered. It was a strange image to pull out of thin air, she couldn't help thinking. "You have any paper and a pencil lying around?" she asked the woman.

The woman opened the door to them for the first time since they'd rung her doorbell. She beckoned them into her apartment, urging them to "C'mon, c'mon, let's get this over with."

Within fifteen minutes, following the description the woman gave her, a sketch of Monica's boyfriend and, according to the neighbor, the father of the dead woman's baby, found its way onto the page.

"Not that he was ever going to do right by her. He was just in it for a good time and the money. Monica had a good heart and a good job. She deserved better." The neighbor sniffed, her eyes growing teary.

"No argument there," Shane agreed.

Taking a look at the drawing that his temporary partner had produced, he had to admit he was impressed. "Pretty good," he told her with an appreciative nod. He had a feeling that if he said anything more effusive, she would simply discount it. The officer, he'd already noted, didn't take compliments well. "You do this on the side? Sketch, paint, that sort of thing?" he asked.

"Not on the side," she contradicted. "But I do it. It relaxes me." She supposed that he would call it a hobby—but it was more than that. Drawing was the gatekeeper to her soul.

He looked down at the sketch again. "Impressive," he told her.

She wasn't accustomed to getting compliments and had no idea how to handle the praise, other than with an indifferent, casual shrug.

"Maybe we should circulate this," she suggested.

He agreed. "And give Brenda a copy of it in case it helps her identify that mystery caller who went into Monica's apartment and never came out." He looked at the woman who had given them the description. "Would you know where he lives?"

"Up until a couple of months ago, with her," she answered flatly.

"Which means, if we're lucky, the guy's name is on the lease," Ashley related out loud. She looked at Shane to see if he agreed.

He did. Shane was grinning. "Maybe you do have a knack for this kind of thing," he told her.

She tried to look completely indifferent to the words of praise, but the tiny hint of a smile gave her away.

Chapter 10

There was a different man in the leasing office this time.

The plastic-looking man glanced up from his desk the moment Shane opened the door and let Ashley enter in front of him. Actually, since the door, as well as the adjacent panels on either side of it, was completely made of glass, allowing for total visibility, the leasing manager, a man in his early thirties, looked up a second *before* the door was fully opened. It was obvious that a movement just outside the door had caught his attention.

By the time the door had shut behind them, the leasing manager had risen from behind his desk and was in the process of swooping down on them, a hawk ready to scoop up unsuspecting prey.

"Good morning," he said warmly. "This must be your lucky day."

Just what was this guy up to? Shane wondered. "How so?" he asked.

"Well, according to my computer, an apartment has just gone vacant. You two can get first crack at it since you're right here. The orientation is just right. Warm in the winter, cool in the summer. You can't go wrong. And the price is a steal."

Since they weren't jumping at the chance to nail down this bargain he was pushing, the man with the shining, slicked-back, overly black hair cocked his head like an attentive bird, studying them. Trying to find a reason they might be dragging their feet.

"Let me guess. This is your first apartment together, right?" he asked.

"It would be," Ashley attested, "if we were looking to lease one, which we're not."

Her answer confused him. "Then why…?" The manager looked from one to the other, waiting to be enlightened by one of them.

"We need to ask you a few questions about the woman who lived in apartment 163," Shane answered.

The dazzling smile instantly vanished as if it had never existed, and was replaced by an annoyed frown. "You're with the police." He said it the way an overly fussy person would have spoken to representatives of the sanitation department.

"Right on the first guess," Shane stated, as if congratulating the manager. Something in his bones told him that the man was going to be less than cooperative.

The manager, Robert Hughes, had a question of his own. "When are you going to take down that awful-looking yellow tape? The residents are beginning to complain about the inconvenience."

"Think of the inconvenience Monica Phillips is going through," Ashley pointed out. Shane noted that she was having trouble hanging on to her temper. He could hear it in the way her voice rose.

"I don't think that tape is an awful shade of yellow, do you?" Shane asked the woman next to him.

Playing along, Ashley shook her head. "Doesn't look awful to me," she replied with sincerity.

Shane turned back toward the leasing manager. "Give it a chance. It'll grow on you," he told the pretentious man.

"When are you taking it off?" Hughes demanded again through clenched teeth.

"Well—Robert," Shane said, reading the man's name from the nameplate on his desk, "that depends on how quickly we can gather up all the available clues in Monica's apartment. One of her neighbors told us that until a few weeks ago, there were two people renting that apartment. Monica and the father of her baby. If he was on the lease, we're going to need all the leasing information you have on him."

Robert drew himself up to his full height—and still fell several inches shy of Shane. "That information is confidential," he informed the two representatives of the police department haughtily.

Shane was not about to back off. "We *need* that confidential information to find him so we can ask him a few questions about his ex-girlfriend."

"You don't have to keep what you have confidential any longer. It's not like he's an undercover spy," Ashley interjected.

The manager remained unmoved. "Privacy is privacy," he recited stubbornly.

"We can always come back with a warrant," Shane told him evenly. It was a threat nonetheless.

Robert crossed his arms defiantly before his chest. "Go ahead," he challenged. By the expression on his face, it was apparent that the leasing manager was fairly confident that all this would lead to nothing.

"Oh, we will," Ashley promised, adding, "Just think of all the inconvenience the residents are going to have to suffer through if we have to bring back a squad of police officers to make sure that nothing is tampered with in the apartment until the warrant is issued and then served. Why, it might even be a whole week before that warrant shows up—"

"All right, all right," the manager cried angrily, throwing up his hands. "I'll get you that name and any information I have on the other tenant." He stormed back to his computer and began to type furiously. The keys echoed the staccato beat.

Less than ninety seconds later Hughes had pulled up the requested information and had printed it.

Muttering something less than charitable under his breath, he stormed over to the printer and retrieved the page with the contact information on it.

"There!" he declared. "Now will you please leave?" The request was fairly bitten off and heavily laced with sarcasm.

"We will. For now," Shane told him as he and Ashley started for the door. "Oh, and thanks for your cooperation."

The door slammed behind them.

Once he and Ashley were outside the office again and on their way back to his vehicle, Shane grinned at her. "Nicely done," he said. "You really knew how to get under his skin."

Ashley shrugged off the compliment. "I've had practice," she said drolly.

"Lucky for me," he commented with a laugh. Unlocking his car, Shane slid into the driver's seat and leaned over to access the onboard computer. "Let's see if this guy's got any outstanding warrants or a criminal history."

A quick search through the database showed that the man, Jordan Simon, didn't have either. The next step was to access DMV records to find both Simon's picture and hopefully his current address—*if* the man had been conscientious enough to update the DMV on his new residence.

Securing that information took a little time as well as patience and, in the end, a little help from Brenda, who wormed her way into a database not readily accessed by the average law-enforcement agent.

"Bingo," Shane declared happily when the information appeared on the screen before him. Brenda had forwarded the information to his car. "Brenda, if you weren't already married to my cousin, I'd run off with you and marry you myself."

"Big talk." Brenda laughed in response. "Now let me get back to my work. This recording you brought me is just possibly the most worn out, grainiest recording I've ever had to work with," she complained with a sigh.

"Keep trying, Brenda," he said encouragingly. "You're the best."

"Yeah, yeah," she replied in a weary, singsong voice just before she terminated the transmission.

Ashley glanced at her oversize watch to check on the time. Between questioning tenants, following up leads and checking back with Brenda, they'd been at this for the better part of the day. It was getting late, certainly way past either one of their usual quitting times. She half expected the detective to call it a night.

Shane saw the petite young officer looking at her watch—which he noted was way too big for her. A gift from a former boyfriend? Or maybe someone who was currently in her life?

That was none of his business, he reminded himself. They were working together, not playing together. And as far as working together, it was getting late. As of yet, there'd been no overtime authorized for this case, and he was sure she probably wanted to go home.

"We can call it a night," he told her.

"You can knock off for the night if you want to," she countered. "Just drop me off at my car."

It wasn't hard for him to read between the lines. "I take it you're not ready to quit," he said.

She knew she could pretend to change her mind and say she was going to go home, but Cavanaugh was too smart to be taken in by that. She might as well play it straight and give him an honest answer.

"I thought I'd just see if this so-called ex-boyfriend has been listening to the news, or if he's the one responsible for *causing* the news."

In that case, he might as well go with her, Shane thought. He started up the car again. There was something about her tone of voice when she said that that put him on the alert. "You made up your mind about him?" He was asking her a question, but he had a feeling he knew the answer to that.

Ashley replied with another question. "That wouldn't be very ethical now, would it?"

"I'm not asking about ethical," Shane said mildly. "I'm asking about you. Are you going to go talk to this guy having already played judge and jury?"

It was hard thinking of Monica's ex-boyfriend as being innocent until proven guilty, but that was the name of the game: impartiality.

She blew out a breath. "Well, he did walk out on

her and the baby, but that could just be a case of responsibility jitters," she pointed out, knowing she was speculating. "Maybe we should stop by my place and I can take Albert with me," she suggested with a smile that was way too innocent to be real. "See what he has to say."

"Now he's a talking dog?" Shane asked as they drove to the address Brenda had secured for them.

If Ashley heard the amusement in his voice, she pretended not to. She took his mocking question as an opportunity to educate him. "All animals talk to you. You just have to listen."

It wasn't a theory he subscribed to, but he let it go for now. All he did was point out the obvious. "The dog just might not like him."

"If he walked out on my pregnant mistress and made her cry, I wouldn't be too crazy about him, either," she said.

"What makes you think she cried over him?" Shane asked, curious where she got her information.

"Easy, his pictures were still up in her apartment. If the breakup was something she orchestrated or was hoping for, or held a grudge against him for, she would have smashed his pictures—or thrown them out. But she displayed them."

"Okay, you made a believer out of me," Shane told her with a laugh.

"Take me back to the precinct," she requested, "so that I can get my car and then—"

"We'll go see this guy together," Shane concluded for her.

He wasn't willing to let her go off on her own, she thought. "Afraid I'll steal your thunder?" she quipped.

"Afraid you might create thunder if you don't hear any," he countered matter-of-factly.

Ashley sat in the passenger seat, silent as she struggled to hang on to her temper. He'd just insulted her. How was she supposed to work with a man who had all but just said she wasn't trustworthy? "Are you doubting my integrity?"

He looked a little mystified as to how she had arrived at the bizarre conclusion. "More like I'm worried about your enthusiasm to bring this guy down no matter what."

"I want to bring down whoever it was who killed that poor woman and stole her baby, nothing more, nothing less," she informed him with feeling. "No matter what you might think of me or my dog catching job, I don't lie, Detective Cavanaugh. Is that understood?" she asked, watching his face intently.

"Understood," he finally replied after more than a minute had gone by.

"Okay, then, step on it," she urged. "Since you obviously don't trust me to do this on my own, let's find this guy before he decides to pick up and disappear for good."

She had a feeling that time was of the essence if they were going to save the baby. She refused to think about the possibility that the infant was dead. Backup had already conducted a thorough search of all the Dumpsters in the area.

"The sooner we get this done," she told him, "the sooner you can get back to your evening."

He laughed shortly as he eased to a stop at an intersection. "Nothing much to get back to."

She found that difficult to believe. The man was, after all, handsome as well as charming. Both attributes were known to attract a swarm of women. He struck her as someone who would want to make the most of that.

"No hot date waiting for you, wondering where you've got to?" she asked.

"No date, hot or otherwise," he told her, easing back on the gas.

She glanced at his profile. She would have thought it would be more rigid than that. The fact that he was alone for the night didn't seem to bother him at all. Why?

Deciding to be up-front with him, she asked, "Is this where I'm supposed to feel sorry for you?"

"No. But if you want to feel sorry for me—"

Here it comes, Ashley thought, bracing herself for practically anything.

"You can feel sorry for me because I've got a mouthy temporary partner who seems to want to turn every other word between us into a fight."

She said nothing to begin with, then eventually, she gave in to his assessment. She *had* been a wee bit thin-skinned and touchy. It came from years of being embroiled in actual verbal assaults—sometimes physical ones, as well. As far as partners went, temporary or otherwise, Shane seemed like a pretty good guy. He deserved a chance, she told herself.

"Point taken," she conceded. "I'm just used to fighting for every single foothold, every step I make. Nothing ever came easy for me."

And the bitterness shows, he couldn't help thinking. Still, pointing it out wasn't a way to make it go away. It would accomplish just the opposite.

When he was certain she was finished and he wouldn't be interrupting her, Shane made the argument for his defense.

"I just want you to keep one thing in mind. I have three sisters, none of whom I have *ever* felt superior to for more than an intoxicating moment. The seven of us were raised by parents who taught us to regard one another as equals—no matter how inferior my sisters thought my three brothers and I were," he added with a grin. "Got it?"

"Got it," she answered and this time, for some reason, she believed that she did.

"You think we can make this snappy?" the handsome, boorish young man asked in response to the two badges that were being held up for his perusal in the doorway of his studio apartment. "I have a date with this really hot model, and she does *not* want to be kept waiting—know what I mean?" He directed the last part to Shane. It was accompanied by a self-satisfied smirk.

He was the type of man, Shane concluded, that women enjoyed scratching their eyes out—with more women standing on the sidelines, applauding.

"We'd like you to answer a few questions," Shane told him. *"Now,"* he intoned as the man opened his mouth again to lodge another protest. "Know what *I* mean?" Shane asked. He looked pointedly at the victim's former boyfriend.

"What's this about?" Simon demanded as he reluctantly allowed them to enter his tiny studio apartment.

Walking in, Ashley noted the scattered clothing on the backs of chairs and the sofa. There was more on the unmade bed. A forlorn pizza box was buried headfirst in the overflowing garbage pail.

"A little cramped, isn't it?" Ashley asked, taking it all in.

"This is just temporary," Simon informed her dismissively. His tone demanded that she back off with those kinds of questions or suffer the consequences.

This is just temporary, he'd said. Until he found another woman to sponge off of, Ashley thought with contempt.

"Ask your questions so I can go, okay?" he insisted. He obviously didn't like the way she was looking at him. As if he were a fascinating train wreck she couldn't seem to draw her eyes away from.

"When did you last see Monica Phillips?" Shane interjected.

Surprise as well as anger crisscrossed his features. "This is about her?" he asked.

"Answer the question, please," Shane instructed firmly.

Simon was too busy being indignant and angry to answer any question directly.

"Look, whatever she's saying, she's lying," he said heatedly. "She's not even my girlfriend anymore. I've been seeing someone new, someone who appreciates me. Allison Sales," he said proudly. "So Monica is just telling you lies."

"She's not telling us much of anything," Ashley countered, wondering if the guy would even care to hear that his former girlfriend had been killed.

"Well, that's a first," he declared tersely, as though spitting out an apparent bad taste in his mouth.

"So is death, for her."

"Yeah. Wait, what? Who's dead?" he demanded after playing back the words he'd just heard Ashley saying to him.

"Who do you think, Einstein?" Shane asked. His hands itched to take a swing at this guy. Just one swing. He was a poor excuse for a human being, and no one would miss him once he was gone.

Annoyed then puzzled, the man's face was a mask of confusion for exactly fifteen seconds before it looked as if his brain had suddenly kicked in. He thought hard for a moment. Ashley wondered if the effort was going to cause him to implode.

"You're not talking about Monica, are you?" he cried, stunned.

Ashley fixed him with a look that dared him to curse. "And if we were?"

"It's not possible," Wilson insisted. "I just talked to Monica a couple of days ago. She was alive then," the genius pointed out. "How can she be dead?"

Shane decided to give him all the details, carefully watching his face as he spoke. "Somebody decided to give her a C-section early—without the benefit of an anesthetic."

Simon's liberally tanned face turned completely pale as he clutched at his stomach.

The next moment, his knees buckled beneath his weight—despite the fact that he was rail thin—and he made it to the kitchen, where he promptly purged the contents of his stomach into the sink.

Shane winced as the image and the smell got to him. He expected to see Ashley react in much the same manner. Instead she followed the man into the kitchen and ran the water until the last of the pungent stomach contents had been sent down the drain.

"Need a minute to pull yourself together?" Shane asked the suspect.

The man couldn't answer. He held his hand up instead, signaling that he couldn't speak for fear of another bout of purging.

It came, anyway.

Shane's eyes met Ashley's. There was a look in them that he couldn't quite fathom—but it didn't appear as if she was loaded for bear any longer, at least, not where this man was concerned.

From the looks of it, he and she had arrived at the same conclusion. But he wasn't the type to count chickens before the nest was even prepared. So instead, he waited for her to be the one to make the statement.

He didn't have a long wait.

"I don't think he's our killer."

Chapter 11

Stepping back from the man they were questioning, Shane motioned for her to follow suit. When she did, he asked, "What makes you think he's innocent?"

Ashley frowned at the wording he used. "I wouldn't exactly call Simon innocent," she returned. There was contempt in her eyes when she glanced over at the retching man. "He's guilty of absolutely reprehensible behavior—but I don't think he killed Monica Phillips." She winced slightly as Simon went through another round of what by now amounted to dry heaves. "*Nobody* throws up on cue like that. Not without two fingers going down their throat or a dose of ipecac."

Shane nodded. "I tend to agree with you," he said. Looking over at their former suspect, he told the man, "We're going now. Do yourself a favor and don't leave town for a while."

Simon made an unintelligible response, his throat obviously raw at this point.

"You realize that this brings us back to square one," Shane told her as they left the victim's former boyfriend's studio apartment.

Ashley chewed on lower lip for a moment. "Not necessarily."

Her assertion caught him off guard. What had he missed? "Okay," he urged. "Enlighten me."

She'd been wrestling with her thoughts about the heinous nature of the crime and why anyone would choose to do it the exact way they had rather than just hit the victim over the head, or better yet, stab her through either the heart or a major artery if they just wanted her dead. The method was very precise. "I think she was killed *for* her baby."

Shane was open to anything. "You mean, like for a black market ring?" he asked. "I don't know. Seems kind of barbaric to me. There are plenty of women willing to give up their unwanted babies, especially if there's any kind of a monetary incentive involved. Sadly, there's no shortage of unwanted babies," he pointed out. "We see those kinds of headlines all the time—Baby Found in Dumpster—that sort of thing."

She was still fairly certain she was right. "The fact that the killer took an unborn baby might mean that it was more personal. I don't think this was a baby meant to be sold. This was one the perp was going to keep, or give to someone close to him or her who might have lost a baby."

As she warmed to her subject—and grew more convinced that she was right—Ashley's voice swelled in volume. "Whoever did this wanted an infant, a baby from 'scratch,' so to speak, so that the perp could raise it from the first moment it drew breath." Her eyes met his, and she could see that he thought her theory had merit. "Could be someone who lost a baby during childbirth, and the need to replace that baby was just too overwhelming to ignore."

Shane looked at her for a long moment. There was something in her voice that caught his attention; that made him think that this was more than just a theory for her. Did she know someone like that, someone who'd lost an infant and had entertained a desperate plan to fill the hole that had to have been left in that person's heart after going through that sort of loss?

"You sound like you're speaking from experience," he said quietly. "Are you?"

For a moment Ashley had lost herself in the past without realizing it. She reconnoitered quickly.

"What? Me? No," Ashley denied quickly and with feeling. "I've just got a large capacity for empathy, that's all."

There was no way she was about to share something as personal as the loss of her baby with him. Nine months of preparing, of coming to terms with the situation of being a single mother and then, near the end, of looking forward to it only to be faced with a cold reality and forced to make the best of it—as if there *was* a best to it—without a drop of emotional support from anyone. Because there had been no one, a fact that, coupled with her loss, had very nearly broken her. But then she'd rallied.

She always rallied.

"Empathy usually means that you've gone through the same thing," Shane told her, his eyes still on hers.

"Sympathy," Ashley said, stressing every syllable of the word. "I meant sympathy." And then her indignation took hold. "Are we trying to solve a murder or correct my word choice?" Ashley asked impatiently.

"Nothing in the handbook that says we can't do both," Shane told her mildly.

Her frustration was beginning to mount. Ashley could feel herself on the edge of an explosion, and no good could come from that. He could easily get her dismissed from the case, and at this point, she felt invested in it.

"You know, you're right," she said with a false brightness. "We should call it a night. I don't know about you, but it's way past my bedtime."

He knew it was all an act—a man didn't grow up with three sisters and remain clueless to such things—but it was also for the best. They were both getting a little punchy, and that was when accidents happened and details got overlooked. His first homicide was way too important to him for him to take any chances that might mess him up.

"Mine, too," he told her. "I'll drive you back to

the precinct so you can get your car, then head on home myself."

Ashley merely nodded in response to his offer. She didn't trust herself to conduct a conversation with him at this point. Her emotions were much too close to the surface, stirred up as they had been by some of the details of this case.

When Shane drove into the precinct's parking lot some twenty minutes later, he absently noted that most of the cars had left for the night. He pulled up beside hers. Unable to wait a second longer, Ashley fairly bolted out of his vehicle.

"See you in the morning?" Shane called after her.

His question caught her by surprise. It also pleased her. Part of her had been braced for a confrontation since she'd thought Cavanaugh would want to handle the rest of the investigation by himself. That he had just assumed she was in it for the long haul was a weight off her shoulders. Her energy would be better spent on the investigation and not on second-guessing him.

However, given what she'd experienced in her formative years—that nothing was ever done altruistically—she was rather suspicious about the detective's motives.

"Sure," she finally answered. "I'll come up to your squad room in the morning." Ashley assumed that Cavanaugh would prefer her coming up to his department rather than his coming down to hers.

That was fine with her. The space in Animal Control was rather limited and austere, even by department standards.

Shane nodded just before he drove away. "Good," he called out.

But Ashley was already getting into her car, and if she heard his last word, she gave no indication.

Shane had no idea what to make of her, but he knew he was ready to try to unravel the mystery that was Ashley St. James. The fact that he wanted to amazed him in itself. After Kitty, he had been certain that he didn't want to approach anything that even remotely felt like a relationship. The intrigued way he felt about Ashley just told him that nothing was carved in stone.

He smiled to himself. His father always encouraged him to remain flexible....

He saw the light immediately.

The light was on in his ground-floor apartment. Shane was positive that he'd turned all the lights off before he'd left this morning.

Which meant that someone was in his apartment.

He never took his eyes off the front door as he pulled his car up into the carport right in front of the apartment.

One hand on his weapon, Shane eased his key into the lock and slowly turned it, taking care not to make any noise as he opened the door.

There *was* someone in his tiny kitchen. He recognized her just as his weapon cleared his holster.

His body, completely rigid and on high alert less than a second earlier, relaxed now as he blew out a long, exasperated breath.

In contrast to his state, the woman in his kitchen glanced over her shoulder and offered him a complacent smile.

"I was beginning to think they were holding you hostage at the precinct. I was all set to call Dad and tell him to go rescue you."

Shane slid his gun back into its holster. "Kari, what the hell are you doing here?"

"And hello to you, too," his sister responded brightly. Kari stepped back from the stove so that he could see for himself what she was doing here. "Obviously your keen eyes of observation are not so keen—another reason you should have come home earlier. Otherwise you would have been able to figure out that I was cooking a late dinner for you."

While he appreciated his sister fussing over him, he didn't like the idea that she thought he *needed* to be fussed over. "You don't have to cook me dinner, Kari, late or otherwise."

"Sure I do," she contradicted. "Otherwise, I won't know if you're eating or not."

He hated the fact that his family kept eyeing him as if they were expecting him to self-destruct or lapse into deep mourning.

"I'm fine, Kari. Really," he insisted. "You don't have to hover over me."

With a dismissive sniff, Kari set the spatula in her hand down on the side of the stove and turned around to face him.

"Haven't you heard? Cavanaughs do *not* hover. We protect, we offer emotional and moral support, but we don't hover like some commercial airplane in a holding pattern."

"Well, you certainly took to waving the Cavanaugh banner pretty quickly," he observed.

Kari shrugged casually, the way she approached and viewed almost everything in life. "It's been ours all along. We just weren't made aware of it. So why not use it?" she asked.

He envied Kari's laidback manner. He emulated it, but with him it was a studied pose, not a genuine reaction the way it was with Kari.

"Well, for the record, you hover," he insisted. "Speaking of hovering, shouldn't you be with that fearless fiancé of yours?"

She didn't see the reason for the adjective. "Fearless?"

"He's marrying you, isn't he?" The question drew a swing from his sister. Her fisted hand connected solidly with his shoulder. Hard enough to get him to vibrate even though he did his best not to. "Which reminds me," he said as he pulled out of reach. "I still have to take him aside and tell him some of the things he can hold over your head whenever you're driving him crazy—which, knowing you, will be pretty much all the time."

"You're my brother," she pointed out. "You're supposed to be loyal to me."

"You don't need any help," he told her. "However, Esteban just might."

She glanced at the fried chicken she'd heaped on a plate, then reached for it. "Maybe I'll just take dinner back with me."

Shane was quicker than she was and caught her hand, stopping her from carrying out the threat. "No, don't. I take it all back. This smells too good to let it escape." He took another deep whiff to underline his point. "But seriously, Kari," he told her, "you can stop worrying. I'm fine."

"Your partner got shot and would have died if you hadn't held his insides in your hand, pressing down to stop the bleeding, and then your fiancée uses this as a reason to walk out on you less than a week before the wedding. How does that make you fine?" she challenged. Before he could offer up any sort of an answer, she pointed out what to her was a glaring fact. "Although I hope you realize that you dodged a bullet. Any woman who puts her needs above those of the man she's supposed to love—a man who clearly needs her in a time of stress—well, in my humble opinion, she doesn't have it in her to make a marriage work."

He laughed. "Since when is anything about you humble?" he asked. "And what makes you such an authority on the subject of marriage? You're not even married yet."

"Yet." She seized on the word he'd used and underscored it. Her wedding to Esteban was not all that far away. "Besides, being in love with a great guy makes me see what a really solid relationship is all about." Kari placed her hand on his shoulder. Her teasing tone had vanished, and there was genuine concern in her eyes now as they met his. "I just wanted to make sure you were okay."

He grinned broadly. "I just caught my very first homicide case. I'm more than fine," he assured her.

"Unlike the victim of the homicide," she countered glibly. She knew better than to push the matter any further now. And maybe he was coming around a little. Work was a great distracter. "Well, seeing as how you're breathing and I just left you a great dinner, I guess that qualifies you as being okay for now." She wiped her hands on a nearby kitchen towel. "So I will be getting back to Esteban." She paused to brush a quick kiss on his cheek. "Call me if you need me."

Shane nodded. "I'll just look out my window and beckon over the first hovering aircraft that I see," he promised.

Kari rolled her eyes. He was impossible. "You don't deserve me."

"You're right," he agreed. Making his way to the door, he opened it for her, his inference crystal clear. "Leave. Make me suffer."

"Idiot." She laughed, cuffing him on the side of his head just before she left.

He *was* lucky, Shane thought as he closed the door after his sister's departing back. Whenever he needed someone, even during the years that he was growing up, there was *always* a parent or sibling to turn to.

Just as there was now.

When Kitty had knocked him for a loop by calling off the wedding and walking out on him that way, everyone in his family rallied around him, forming a tight circle about him as if they were trying to keep anything bad from coming through.

He thought of what Ashley had mentioned to him earlier—most likely unintentionally, given what a private person she was—about bouncing from one foster home to another when she wasn't being sent back to the group home. She was clearly in distress at being so alone, and her withdrawing from the world was her way of dealing with it. She was all but acting out a scenario with dialogue that fairly screamed, "You don't want me, fine. I don't want you more."

How had she done it? How had she managed to survive a childhood like that? And then wound up wanting to be a cop? The sort of upbringing she'd had—or lack thereof—produced closet psychos and sociopaths, sometimes without the benefit of a closet.

He realized that he was feeling sorry for her.

The next moment, as he helped himself to a crisply fried chicken leg from the platter his sister had left for him, Shane couldn't help but laugh. He had a hunch that if Ashley even *suspected* that he felt sorry for what she'd had to go through, she would probably wind up handing his head to him.

Literally.

Preoccupied, he took a bite of the fried chicken Kari had prepared for him, and his attention immediately focused on the happy explosion of flavor taking place in his mouth and on his tongue. Damn, but that was good.

If he was any judge, it looked as if Kari took after their newly discovered Uncle Andrew, who was famous for his impromptu spreads, the ones that were rumored to be able to feed untold masses.

Apparently cooking was in the genes, even if those genes were unaware of their connection to the Cavanaugh dynasty until just the past year.

Shane ate a few more pieces of chicken with relish, but even as he quickly consumed what was on his plate, he couldn't help but wonder if Ashley was eating alone, or if she even bothered to eat dinner. Was her cupboard only filled with dog food? After spending the day together, she struck him as someone who made a habit of putting herself last.

It occurred to him as he cleared off his table and put the dishes into the compact dishwasher that he was really looking forward to seeing her again.

When he walked into the squad room the next morning, he found that Ashley was already there. He really wasn't all that surprised. He supposed he was somewhat surprised that she hadn't just stayed here last night. But a change of clothes—she was wearing civilian clothing rather than her uniform—told him that she'd gone home, at least for a little while.

Since she was on temporary loan from her department, for the moment replacing his wounded partner, his captain had put her at his partner's desk. He figured that once either his partner was back, or he and Ashley solved the homicide—whichever came first—Ashley would be back to driving around, searching for strays.

He didn't know if the idea bothered him or not. He supposed he'd figure it out after they spent some more time together.

"You're here bright and early," he commented, placing the cup of tea he'd gotten for himself on his desk and holding out the other one to her.

When she looked at it quizzically but made no effort to accept the offering, he told her, "Take it. It's tea, not a bomb."

Reaching over, she accepted the container. "Why are you bringing me tea?"

"I figured it was the fastest way to administer poison," he quipped, deadpan, then asked her his own question. "Why do you think?"

She regarded the warm container in her hands in silence for a moment, then mumbled something that sounded suspiciously like "Thanks" as she removed the lid. A small scented plume rose from the container like a tiny smoke signal. The contents beneath smelled faintly like vanilla.

Seeing Shane walk in and having him offer her the cup of tea had temporarily made her forget what she'd uncovered by being on the computer for the past hour. She wasn't accustomed to being on the receiving end of anything but grief.

Remembering, she announced, "I found her next of kin." When Shane greeted her words with a blank look, she quickly elaborated. "Our involuntary C-section. Monica Phillips. I found her parents. Or, more accurately," she amended, "I found her father."

Shane sank into the chair at his desk. The thought of what lay ahead of him was more than a little daunting. He'd never had to inform a next of kin about the death of a loved one before. It wasn't an experience he was looking forward to by any stretch of the imagination. "I forgot about that."

"About what?" Ashley queried. Judging by his expression, whatever he was referring to wasn't good, she thought.

"About notifying the next of kin about what's happened."

That had to rank as the least favorite duty of any detective: telling parents that their child's eyes were never going to open again, never look at them with love again, she thought. And she could relate.

Finding out had very nearly broken her.

"I'll go with you," Ashley heard herself saying.

Chapter 12

Her offer to come along surprised him.

As did the feeling of relief that came almost simultaneously.

"Okay, let's go, if you're determined to come with me." Shane pushed his chair away from his desk and rose to his feet. About to walk out, he glanced over his shoulder. Ashley had made no move to follow him. Had she changed her mind about coming along after all?

A closer look at her face told him that mentally, she appeared to be miles away. "You okay?"

The question broke through the layers of years that had temporarily closed in on her. Ashley blinked and tossed her head, shaking off the memories that only served to hurt her heart.

"Sure," she answered a bit too cheerfully. "Why wouldn't I be?"

"You had this strange expression on your face," Shane told her. "Like for a second, you weren't here at all."

She was going to have to work on her poker face, Ashley upbraided herself, waving his words away with a careless gesture.

"Just thinking." Ashley pulled out the small, thin messenger bag she'd deposited into the bottom drawer and slung it over her shoulder. "You want me to go tell the father?" she offered.

Shoulders braced, she reminded him of a soldier about to go into battle. It was obvious to him that she hadn't heard what he'd just said when he'd gotten up. She really had been a million miles away. He couldn't help wondering where that was—and exactly what had triggered her sudden journey.

"No, I'm primary on this, that's my job," he told her, much as he hated the thought of what he had to do. But if he wanted to work in Homicide, it was all part of the territory. He might as well get used to it. Still, her offer did make him curious as to what had motivated it. "Why? You want to do it?"

"I'm willing," she said, deliberately sidestepping a direct answer to his question.

He laughed shortly as they headed out of the squad room. There was very little humor in the sound. "Get much practice by telling people their pets have been flattened?"

She looked very serious as she replied, "No, not really."

Why would someone volunteer to take on something so spirit-crushing if they didn't have to do it, or had at least grown immune to doing it? He needed an answer. Maybe that would begin to unlock the puzzle that Officer Ashley St. James clearly was.

"Then why?"

She shrugged carelessly, avoiding his eyes as she pushed the down button for the elevator. Why couldn't the man just accept help and not try to examine it under a microscope? "Because you looked as if it would really bother you to have to do it."

So this was just an act of charity on her part? Again, why? "And it wouldn't bother you?"

The elevator doors opened. She went in, turned around and pressed the button for the first floor, still avoiding his eyes. "It would, but I've learned how to block out whatever bothers me," she told him.

He supposed that was as good an answer as any. In any event, he sensed it was the only one he was getting. "Thanks, but no. It's my job. I'll do it." He saw her slant a glance in his direction. Unless he missed his guess, she was probably having second thoughts about going along. "But I wouldn't mind a little moral support accompanying me," he added, hitting the ball into her court.

Ashley nodded, understanding his meaning. He was asking her to come along without actually *ask-*

ing her to come along. "One dose of moral support coming up," she promised.

"Now I just need the address—" He never got a chance to finish.

"Way ahead of you," she announced, holding up the page she'd printed a few minutes before he'd walked into the squad room.

He took it from her, glancing at the address she'd tracked down, thanks to the DMV. "Lake Ellsinore?" he said. That was more inland, to the east of where Aurora was located.

"I guess to someone from there, Aurora's like the big city," Ashley mused, one side of her mouth going up in a half smile. The elevator brought them to the ground floor and opened. They walked toward the rear exit and the larger parking lot. "One helpful thing. According to what I could find out, her father's a minister."

He didn't quite see her reasoning. "Why is that especially helpful?" He truly wanted to know.

"Well, if her father's a man of the cloth, his religion will help him through this—or at least, it should. That in turn should make our job—your job," she amended, "a little easier. You know, God's will and all that."

They walked out of the building. The morning sky looked ominous and the air smelled like rain, which was highly unusual, given that it was September, when the devil winds blew in from the desert and everything felt as if it was on the verge of possibly bursting into flames. This was ordinarily the worst part of the fire season.

"We'll see," he told her.

She found that rather a strange answer, given that he seemed like the optimist in this partnership. "You don't think it will?" she asked as they went down the back steps.

Shane had come across a few less than kind-hearted men of God. "Let's just say that all men of the cloth were not created equal."

"Don't care for them?" Ashley ventured, following him to where he parked his sedan.

"I didn't say that," he pointed out, correcting her impression. "I've got an uncle who's a priest and one of the finest men I know, but there's no cookie cutter out there, turning out ministers and priests with Uncle Adam's qualities."

She was far from an expert on the members of the Cavanaugh dynasty, but she thought she would have picked up on this fact. "I didn't know there were any Cavanaughs in the priesthood," Ashley said, surprised.

"There aren't," he told her. "Uncle Adam is a Cavelli." Stopping at the sedan, he glanced at her as he opened the driver's-side door. "Don't tell me you haven't heard the story about my father." It seemed to him that *everyone* at the precinct had heard it, quite possibly everyone in the state since the circumstances were rather unusual and it had been carried as a human interest story in some of the local papers.

"Okay, I won't tell you," she replied cavalierly. "But just so you know, I had no idea which Cavanaugh your father was before yesterday. I don't follow the news much," she admitted.

At least she wasn't trying to dazzle him with her familiarity with his family, he thought, which was a point in her favor. Too many people inside the department tried to make it appear that they knew everything there was to know about his family members, both new and old. Nothing turned him off faster than that.

"My dad was accidentally switched at birth in the hospital with another infant whose first name was Sean and whose last name was Cavelli—same first three letters," he pointed out. "Story goes that the nurse who was responsible for the switch was grieving over the death of her fiancé and didn't realize her mistake."

"So you grew up thinking you were part of one family when you were actually part of another?"

She certainly had a gift for summarizing things, he thought, amused. "That's it in a nutshell," he told her. "The whole thing came to light when people kept mistaking Dad for the former chief of police."

"At least you always had a family around you, no matter what their name was," she concluded.

Shane wondered if she knew that she sounded wistful. He didn't need to be told how lucky he was; he knew. "Look, I didn't mean to sound like I was bragging—"

"You weren't," she told him, cutting short any apology he thought he owed her. "You were just answering questions I was asking. Guess I'm just trying to sharpen some of my investigative skills," Ashley quipped. Getting into the vehicle, she buckled up. "This is a change from my usual day. There's no one to talk to in the van when I'm driving around. I spend most of my time looking for strays and skittish animals that darted into the street at the wrong time." She flashed a half smile at him, summarizing the difference in their work for the department. "You keep the streets safe, I keep them clean—someone's got to pick up the roadkill," she pointed out when he looked at her quizzically.

He raised a shoulder, executing a half shrug. "Never thought about it that way," he admitted.

"Most people don't."

There was no belligerence in her voice.

The trip to Lake Ellsinore was hypnotically tedious. Part of the trip was on a winding, two-lane road.

While Shane drove, she continued researching the Reverend Horace Phillips on the tablet she had unofficially "borrowed" for the road trip. Among other things, she found out that the Church of the Sacred Way was a weathered-looking building still standing on the spot where it had originally been constructed close to eighty years ago. Its congregation was small but fiercely devoted, and Monica's father had been its only shepherd for the past thirty-one years.

Ashley relayed each find to the man in the driver's seat as it came up.

"Amazing what you can get off the internet these days," she commented.

"Especially since the homes in the area look as if they're lucky to have running water," Shane observed. He was surprised she was getting a signal on the electronic device. The houses they'd passed in the past four miles looked like they belonged to a farming community—without the farms. He glanced in her direction, nodding his head at the houses they were passing. "I get an eerie vibe. How about you?"

She looked up from the tablet and focused on the immediate area they were traveling through. She doubted that the town where the victim's parents lived had more than three hundred people.

"All I can say is that it's lucky for me I'm not into this zombie craze that's going around lately, but yes, this place gives me the creeps," she said succinctly. There was a woman standing in the doorway of a house as they passed, just staring as they drove by. "It's the kind of place they must have used to film *The Children of the Corn*."

The reference took him completely by surprise. "You an old movie buff?" he asked.

"Not so much of a buff," she countered—she couldn't quote lines or anything like that, "but I watched a lot of old movies when I was growing up. Not much to do when you have no friends," she said offhandedly.

Did she have any idea how isolated that sounded? "Why didn't you have any friends?"

She stared straight ahead, trying to focus on the terrain around them and not on the past. But it felt as if the past was always hovering over her, like a slick mist she couldn't escape.

"Hard to make friends when you don't know if you're going to be someplace a week from now," she told him. "Easier all around if you just keep to yourself."

"Must have made having a birthday party hard," he commented, thinking back to the friends he'd had as a kid, the parties he'd attended.

The shrug was careless, the tone deliberately distant. "I wouldn't know."

"You never had a birthday party?" he asked, surprised. A birthday party, no matter how small, was something he'd taken for granted as being a right for every kid, no matter how poor. One of his favorite gifts had been a sweater his mother had made for him. He'd worn it until it completely came apart at the seams. It was the love behind the parties and the gifts that counted, not the actual presents themselves.

Open mouth, insert foot, he upbraided himself.

"I never had a birthday," she told him in the same distant voice.

Okay, now she was exaggerating. "Everyone has

a birthday—unless you're an immortal," Shane said with a laugh.

She turned toward him then, her eyes meeting his. "If you have no identity, you can't have a birthday," Ashley said simply. "And social services never found out who I was."

That didn't make any sense. "But they had to have. You've got a last name," he pointed out.

The corners of her mouth curved in an ironic smile. "St. James? Like it?" she asked. Then, not waiting for a response, she told him, "I made it up. James was inscribed on the back of this watch they found on me. I figured it belonged to my father and that James was his name. Anyway, St. James sounded kind of special, and there was nobody to say that it *wasn't* my name, so I kept it. I made it legal when I turned eighteen."

From the little he'd learned about her, not searching for her roots seemed against type. "Weren't you ever curious about your background?"

"Sure."

That was more like it. "And?" he prompted.

"And nothing," she said flatly. "I gave it a shot, went to the local newspapers, asked to look into their archives, went on the internet, all that good stuff." There was a mocking note in her voice as she recalled the enormous frustration she'd dealt with. "Had a few false leads that took me nowhere and finally decided I could spend my time better. So I stopped beating my head against dead ends and put my energy toward improving my marketable skills."

"What sort of 'marketable skills'?" He wanted to know, finding himself more and more curious about the woman fate had had cross his path. More and more attracted to her, as well, and not just her looks, but also the character that was emerging out of these ashes he kept encountering.

"I can tie a knot in a cherry stem with my tongue," she said, a deadpan expression on her face. Then, when she saw the incredulous look on his face, she had to laugh. "God, you should see your face."

She was having fun at his expense, Shane realized. He shrugged, supposing that maybe he deserved that. "I take it you're kidding."

"Oh no, I can do it," she assured him with a toss of her head. "But I'd have to be really simple-minded to count that as a skill. I made myself more marketable by taking a few criminology courses at the local two-year college. Thought maybe someday, when I moved on from Animal Control, those courses might come in handy.

"This must be the place," she commented as they pulled up to the church. It looked even worse for wear in reality than it did on the internet. "According to the address from the DMV, it looks like Monica's parents live behind it."

She said parents, but in actuality, all she'd found so far was information about the victim's father. Not a single word about her mother. Could the woman be gone? Dead, perhaps? If she was, that would have given her something in common with the victim, Ashley thought grimly. They'd both been motherless.

He and Ashley got out of his sedan practically at the same time. Shane went ahead and knocked on the door. The house looked as if it was just a few years younger than the church whose shadow it stood in.

Getting no response, Shane knocked again. He knocked a total of three times before the door to the narrow, two-story wood-framed building finally opened.

A somewhat heavyset man with a cloud of pure white hair came out. He had on the traditional minister's collar and an untraditional frown as he looked them over critically. The minister pointed to something in the distance just before he began to speak. "The main road is three miles due east. Follow it, and it'll take you to the freeway—eventually."

The man obviously thought they were looking for directions. "We're not lost, Reverend," he told the man gently, working his way up to what he had to say. And the questions he wanted to ask.

Impatience creased the overly high forehead. "Then who are you, and what are you doing here?" the minister asked.

He and Ashley took out their badges and IDs at the same time, holding them up as he told the minister their names.

"As to what we're doing here," Shane continued,

"I'm sorry to have to be the one to have to tell you this, but your daughter Monica is dead."

"Yes, she is," the minister said flatly with no emotion.

Stunned, Ashley stared at the man. "Wait, you know she's dead?" There was no way he could have found out. The story was being kept from the local news media pending the next-of-kin notification. All details had been concealed.

Had the story leaked? All the way up here?

Rather than appearing stunned or deliberately controlled, the minister looked angry. "I said so, didn't I?" he snapped.

"Would you mind telling us how you happen to know that, Reverend?" Shane asked.

It was obvious that the man was struggling to keep his temper under wraps, but he looked on the verge of lashing out.

"She is disobedient, she is a fornicator and she is with child," he stormed, enumerating each point harshly. "That makes her dead to me, to the community and most of all, dead to the Giver of Life to us all."

"She is also dead to everyone else, sir," Shane told the minister. He was doing his best to keep his contempt in check. Not for the daughter, but for the father who seemed so indifferent to the daughter he was being told he'd lost. "As in, without any vital signs. Someone killed your daughter, Reverend." He watched the man's face as he spoke. "She was found butchered on her kitchen floor." With each word he added, Shane intently studied the minister's expression. It only seemed to harden more.

How could a man call himself a father and listen to something that should be heartbreaking without displaying an inkling of any real emotion?

"As is to be expected from a fornicator," the minister declared. "The Lord's justice is swift."

Shane's eyes narrowed. *What a coldhearted bastard. No wonder your daughter ran off as soon as she could.* "You mind us asking where you were Monday night through Tuesday morning?"

The reply came after several moments. It was obvious that the minister did not care to have to volunteer his whereabouts. "Tending my flock, as always."

Yeah, right. "Can any of your 'flock' verify this, Reverend?" Ashley asked.

The minister turned on her, a look of pure anger in his eyes. "Are you accusing me?"

"Let's just say we're trying to rule you out," Shane answered, deliberately moving his body between the minister and Ashley. The man didn't look above striking out at someone weaker than he was.

"The Lord will punish you, too, for this," the minister railed at them.

"No doubt," Shane agreed glibly. "But in the meantime, I still need the name or names of any of your 'flock' who can vouch for your whereabouts."

"This is outrageous!" the reverend shouted.

"No, this is procedure, sir," Ashley countered,

her tone as mild as his was loud. She sensed that it goaded the man. "The names?" she prompted, waiting.

Condemning their "godless souls to eternal damnation"—the reverend failed to see the irony in that—he wrote down the names of several people, then thrust the paper at Shane. He refused to even look at the woman with him. "They were all at the prayer meeting. The last one's my wife."

Shane glanced over the names. "We'll be speaking to all of them," he assured the minister.

"When?" the minister demanded.

"Now," Shane replied. "Before anyone can talk to them."

The man's face turned an intriguing shade of red. "You're questioning my word?"

"We're the police. We question everything," Ashley told him glibly. "By the way," she added as they walked out of the building, "we're very sorry for your loss." She knew the words were useless in this case, but she said them, anyway. For the dead woman's sake.

The next moment she regretted making the effort.

"It's no loss," the minister snapped.

"Whatever you say," she replied, then pressed her lips together to keep from saying anything further—or telling the man what she thought of him.

"Don't you even want to ask about the baby?" Shane inquired.

The minister shrugged. "I'm assuming it perished

with her. Just as well," he concluded, turning away. "It's the devil's spawn."

"Let's get out of here," Shane said to Ashley. "The air smells pretty putrid in here." Then he looked back at the minister. "We'll let you know when you can come for your daughter's body. The medical examiner hasn't released it yet."

The minister looked at him as if he couldn't understand why he was being given this information. "Tell him to do whatever he wants with the body," he ordered them. "I have no daughter."

Shane knew he should just ignore the angry minister and walk away. But he couldn't let the man's words go without some sort of comment. "It's easy to see that she certainly had no father."

He walked away with the minister sputtering indignantly in the background. Being around someone like that made him appreciate his family even more. Out of the corner of his eye, Shane saw that Ashley was smiling. It softened her features, transforming her into a far more approachable, not to mention alluring, young woman.

"You know what?" Ashley said to him the moment they got away from the toxic minister.

"What?"

"At least the minister did one good deed," she said as she stood beside the sedan.

He had no idea what she was talking about. "How do you figure that?"

"For the first time in my life, my childhood doesn't seem so bad," she said, punctuating her words with a dry laugh.

Chapter 13

"I'm beginning to think that Monica's father is far more likely to have killed Monica than that worthless boyfriend of hers," Shane commented as he opened his door.

Ashley had to agree with him. Of the two men, the minister struck her as the more heartless one. "Could be Reverend Phillips heard the words of God whispering in his ear, telling him to punish Monica for her transgressions."

Shane nodded. "That sounds like something he would say. Let's find out if the good reverend's alibi holds up," he said pragmatically.

"It might hold," Ashley admitted. "But there is definitely nothing good about the reverend."

"Amen to that." And then he grinned when he saw the way Ashley rolled her eyes. "No pun intended."

"Yeah, right." Getting into the sedan, she buckled up and then waited for him to get in on his side and do the same. "There's just one problem with all this," she said once Shane was in the car.

"What?"

"What did he do with the baby? Given the way he feels about the fact that she got pregnant, why would he bother separating it from his daughter's body?" That bothered her. She would have thought that if the reverend had killed his daughter, he would have left them together, not being able to stomach the sight of his daughter *or* her child.

"That's something to look into once we establish whether or not his alibi checks out. My guess is that since he considered the baby the devil's spawn, he either buried it or threw it somewhere where it could never be found." He started up his car. "Okay, let's see if the reverend even knows *how* to tell the truth."

Three hours later they discovered that not only did the minister know how to tell the truth, but apparently he had. According to several members of his faithful flock, Reverend Phillips was indeed at the prayer meeting as he'd claimed. He was the one conducting the meeting, expounding on the evils of a thankless child.

"Bet Christmas was a barrel of laughs in the Phillips's household," Shane commented. They'd already discovered that the reverend's wife, Monica's mother, had left him shortly after their daughter had run away from home.

The moment the words were out of his mouth, Shane realized that the woman with him had no yardstick to go by when it came to what could be regarded as a good Christmas, and that his reference probably just drove that home for her.

"Sorry," Shane apologized quietly.

"For what?" Ashley asked. As far as she was concerned, he hadn't said anything he needed to apologize for, at least not recently.

Shane spelled it out for her as he put the church and the community behind them. It was a shrinking image in his rearview mirror. "For forgetting that you don't have a frame of reference when it comes to Christmas."

She surprised Shane by contradicting him. "Sure I do."

All right, he was officially confused now. Ashley had good memories when it came to the holidays, but she hadn't experienced something as personal as a birthday celebration? That didn't make any sense to him.

"I don't understand," he told her. "You said you had no family."

She stared straight ahead, out the window. "I didn't. I don't. But that doesn't mean I don't have a frame of reference. I have *It's A Wonderful Life,* and I watched *Home Alone* at least half a dozen times. Just because I never had one of my own, I still know what the right kind of Christmas is supposed to be like."

Ashley thought for a moment. "There was this one year that this Marine came to the group home," she recalled. "He was dressed as Santa Claus, but he was using padding and a fake beard and you could see that underneath all that, he was actually a young guy. The padding had moved by the time he was finished," she recalled with a fond smile on her face. "The other kids in the room all believed he was the real deal, and I was going to say something to set them straight."

"Did you?" he asked.

Ashley shook her head.

"Why not?" Given the fact that she was exceedingly keen on following the straight and narrow path, he would have bet that she would have felt she was striking a blow for truth by exposing the fake Santa Claus. And yet she hadn't; she'd allowed the myth to continue.

Why?

If she closed her eyes, Ashley could almost see the scene unfolding before her. "Because Santa looked into my eyes, and at that moment, I realized that if I said anything, I'd be ruining Christmas for a bunch of little kids who needed hope, not truth, so I didn't say anything. That was *my* Christmas present to them."

Shane laughed and shook his head. "You were a complicated person even then, weren't you?"

Ashley shrugged. She'd never thought of herself as being particularly complicated. She just was who she was, a woman with no pretenses.

"I had a lot of time on my hands. I had to entertain myself somehow. Now what?" she asked, deftly changing the conversation back to the reason they were way out here in the first place. "Since her father has an alibi and wasn't carrying out the wrath of God, that takes us back to square one for a second time. How many times can we keep doing that?"

"As many times as we need to until we get it right," he told her pragmatically. "We haven't interviewed Monica's coworkers yet. Maybe she confided in one of them, mentioned something about being followed or, more specifically, being stalked."

"A stalker?" Ashley questioned, turning the idea over in her head. "You think a stalker did this to her? Is that what you're going with?"

"Until something better comes along," he answered. "But I take it by your tone that you don't." There was a tanker truck in front of them. He sped up to get around it before the road narrowed and he was stuck behind it for the next forty or fifty miles. "Okay, what do you think happened?"

She really didn't have a working theory yet, and that frustrated her. "I think that Monica Phillips had a terrible childhood, and then just when things looked to be turning around for her, she came to a tragic end." Hence the adage that life wasn't fair, she thought, blowing out a breath. "Whoever did this to her, if they had to kill someone, it should have been her father, not her."

"Agreed," Shane responded. "But not exactly the viewpoint we're supposed to embrace," he pointed out, although he had to admit that he found her position somewhat amusing as well as unorthodox.

"Sorry," she murmured more to herself than to him, "it's all I've got at the moment."

"Which is why we're going to talk to Monica's coworkers," he told her. "Maybe they can shed some light on the situation, help us put together the pieces of her life. Tell us if they knew if there was anyone new in the picture."

It turned out that Monica had worked at Baby Mine, the exclusive boutique that had provided most of the baby furniture and stuffed animals that she had in her apartment, rather than shopped there. Abigail Reynolds, the manager, was a warm, maternal-looking woman who had a gift for immediately making anyone who walked through the doors of her charming little baby boutique feel welcomed.

Mistaking them for a couple shopping for their first baby on the way, the woman immediately backtracked when they told her their purpose for being there. She looked genuinely appalled when they gave her the real reason that Monica hadn't showed up for work the past three days.

Abigail looked around her shop, shaking her head. "I don't know how I'm going to break the news to the girls. They all loved her." Her eyes misted over as she told them, "Nicole was going to throw her a baby shower next week." She paused for a moment, trying to get herself under control. "They were all just as excited about that baby as Monica was. Hard to say who was more eager for it to be born, Monica or the rest of the girls who work here."

"And she wasn't resentful?" Shane asked, carefully watching the woman's face to see if she was telling the truth.

"'Resentful'?" the woman echoed, then laughed sadly. "There wasn't a resentful bone in that girl's body. The baby was all she talked about—and I mean *all*. Every penny she made, if she didn't use it to buy food or pay her rent, she would put toward buying something for the baby. I was at her apartment just last week, and I swear that it looked like an annex for the store," the woman told them, gesturing around the show room for emphasis.

"Even with the employee discount, that must have totaled up to a pretty penny," Ashley intoned. She'd glanced at a price tag or two. These were not bargain-basement prices.

"I'll say," the manager readily agreed, "but Monica said she wanted this baby to have everything that she didn't." Abigail moved in closer so that she could lower her voice, mindful of being overheard by the customers. "She didn't talk too much about her childhood, but I gathered her father wasn't the kind people voted Father of the Year."

"Not even if he was the only father left standing," Ashley assured the older woman. She saw the look that Shane gave her and knew she had perhaps spoken out of turn. She didn't care. After the way the reverend had talked about his own deceased daughter, she wasn't concerned about tarnishing the man's precious reputation.

"Would you know if she'd recently seen her father or anyone she knew from her childhood?" Shane asked. Alibi or not, he wasn't a hundred percent certain that the reverend didn't have a hand in his daughter's murder.

Abigail shook her head. "As far as I knew, her father didn't even know where she lived, much less that she was pregnant."

"He did," Ashley told her. "The words he used weren't very flattering."

"From what I heard, I gathered that her father was some kind of religious fanatic," a second woman said, joining them at the side of the store. "Is this about Monica?" the woman whose name tag read Dorothy asked. "Is she okay? She hasn't been answering her phone."

"Monica's dead," the manager told her. "Someone killed her."

Dorothy looked horror-stricken. She covered her mouth to muffle the cry of protest that rose to her lips.

"Was she particularly close to anyone here?" Shane asked the two women.

"She was friendly with everyone," the manager told them. "But I don't think she was closer to one person more than another."

There were tears sliding down the younger woman's cheeks. "She always had a smile and a good word for everyone."

Abigail nodded to confirm the other woman's statement. "I had customers coming in, asking specifically for her because she seemed to take such a personal interest in them." She pressed her lips together to control a momentary loss of composure. "If you ask me, the poor thing was hungry to connect with people, with families." She looked at the other woman as she said this. Dorothy nodded in agreement.

Maybe there was something to go on here, Shane thought. "Would you mind giving us a list of your clientele? Just the ones who would ask for her."

A somewhat skeptical frown furrowed the manager's brow. "Nothing personal, and I would really love to help find whoever did this terrible thing to Monica, but I can't have my customers thinking that I allowed them to be harassed. They'll stop coming here if they believe that," she explained.

Shane was about to say something to try to convince the woman to change her mind, but Ashley was faster. "If these customers specifically asked for Monica, then they had to really like her," she pointed out. "And they would want to find whoever did this to her, don't you think?"

The manager exchanged looks with Dorothy. The latter nodded vigorously, agreeing with what had just been said. Abigail relented, won over by the argument.

"I guess you have a point," she agreed. "All right. Wait right here, and I'll get the names from our computer and print them up for you," Abigail promised.

"That would be great," Ashley told the woman. She retreated, with Dorothy following quickly in her wake, still looking shell-shocked.

As they waited, she could feel Shane looking at her. The moment they were alone, Ashley met his gaze. "Did I do something wrong?" she asked.

"No, on the contrary, you did something very right," Shane answered with an enthusiasm he didn't try to hide. "I was very impressed. You've got good instincts and the makings of a really good detective, Ashley."

Compliments weren't something she was acquainted with or comfortable receiving. For the most part, if anyone addressed a comment to her, it was usually criticism, not praise. As a result, she didn't know how to respond to positive comments—or to Shane.

So she did what she usually did when she felt out of her depth. She mounted a defense.

"Is this where I'm supposed to insert the words *thank you?*" she asked him flippantly.

Instead of answering her or ending the conversation, Shane turned the tables on her and countered with his own question. "Why do you do that?"

"Do what?" she challenged, digging up anger to use as a layer of protection.

"Why do you get sarcastic or defensive whenever I say something nice to you?" he asked her. "If you're having trouble recognizing it, I'm trying to give you a compliment."

"Don't try," she retorted, zeroing in on the word and pretending to find it offensive. "I don't need compliments."

He wasn't buying it. "Everyone needs compliments," Shane told her. "Because everyone needs to feel that they're appreciated."

She lifted her chin. "I don't."

Then, to put some distance between them, thinking that he couldn't follow her, she wandered through the store, glancing at the various items. The price tags were enough to give her sticker shock.

Contrary to what she'd thought, Shane *was* following her around. He shook his head in response to her denial. "You might be fooling yourself, Ashley, but you're not fooling me. I'd say that you need to feel appreciated more than most people because you've never felt that anyone did appreciate you."

She frowned but continued to try to put distance between them. It proved to be fruitless. Shane just kept on following her. "I think you should stick to solving the case and leave the armchair psych 101 stuff to someone else."

"No armchair psych," he countered mildly. "Just common sense."

The manager reappeared with a list in her hand that she held out to him. Accepting it, Shane thanked the woman.

Abigail waved her hand at his words. "You can thank me by telling them that one of your computer techs got it from some cyber database and not me," she requested, lowering her voice so that the two customers near the front didn't overhear her. "We have a decent-size clientele, but in these rough times, we can't afford to lose *any* of our customers—which just might happen if they find out that their privacy has been invaded."

"Everyone's privacy has been invaded," Shane pointed out, folding the paper and placing it into his coat pocket. "Everything's accessible with a little effort. You just made it easier for us. But don't worry, we'll be discreet. My partner here is the last word in discretion," he attested, nodding at Ashley.

The manager smiled and looked as if she was somewhat relieved. "Now get that son of a bitch who killed that poor baby," she instructed.

"Why did you tell that woman that I was your partner?" Ashley asked the moment they were out of the boutique.

He looked mildly surprised by the question. "Because right now, you are. And who knows? The way the department plays musical partners these days, you might very well be my partner once this plays out."

Shane had called his partner, currently on disability, a number of times since the shooting to see how he was doing and also to inform him that the wedding was off.

Wilson had commiserated with him over the blow. The last call had come from him, and he had let Shane know that he might not be coming back after all. His wife was afraid that the next time he was shot, he'd wind up lying in a coffin, not a hospital bed.

"I'm sorry to do this to you, Shane. I really am, but LouAnne's insistent." He'd paused during that last call and then went on to say, "You and me had a really good thing going there for a while, didn't we?"

Never one to give up easily, Shane had said, "Well, don't play taps on the partnership just yet." But even as he'd said it, he'd had a feeling that the final curtain on their collaboration was coming down.

Fast.

"Maybe so," Ashley was saying to him now, regarding his belief that she could wind up being his partner. "But I've got a long way to go toward getting my shield."

"Maybe not as long a way as you think. I've got some pull with the chief of D's," he told her with a wink.

She didn't know all that much about the people

who ran the department, but she did know this. "He doesn't do shortcuts," she pointed out.

At least, that was what she'd heard. According to everyone, Brian Cavanaugh was a man of integrity who couldn't be bribed or threatened into doing anything. It had to come from his sense of honor. She could live with that.

More importantly, she could even admire that.

"No, he doesn't do shortcuts," Shane agreed. "But he does keep an eye on the men and women he thinks have more potential than the rest of the officers. You wouldn't be temporarily filling a detective's spot if you were just average or adequate at your job."

She sincerely doubted that the chief even knew her name, much less anything else about her.

"But I'm in Animal Control," she reminded him, and they both knew what the rest of the departments thought of the people who worked in Animal Control—that they were just a little better than trained chimpanzees. She didn't have to go into detail.

"Yeah," he agreed, a deadpan expression on his face. "And a lot of the people you'll be dealing with are animals."

Ashley laughed then and, as before, he found that he liked the way that sounded and the way it softened her features. Each time that happened, he found her even more appealing than the last time.

Because they were stopped at a light, Shane was able to look at her for longer than if they were moving. He took full advantage of the opportunity.

"Trying to memorize my features so you can pick me out of a line-up?" she asked, still looking straight ahead through the windshield. The countryside was beautiful, but after a bit, its sameness was growing to be somewhat monotonous.

"No, just trying to memorize what you look like when you're actually smiling, since you don't seem to do that very often."

"There's a reason for that. I haven't found all that much to smile about in the past twenty-five years," she told him matter-of-factly.

It wouldn't be until much later that Shane realized that that was the moment he decided it was his mission in life to change that for her.

Chapter 14

The woman in the nursery sat in the rocking chair, her body hunched forward, curled almost into a ball. She was struggling against defeat. Struggling to rise above the noise assaulting her.

Her hands were over her ears, covering them.

It didn't help.

She could still hear it. Still hear the crying. The endless, pathetic crying.

She didn't want to feel this way, didn't want to feel the anger that was bubbling up inside her, ready to spill out. But the sobbing infant was giving her no choice.

And no rest.

She hadn't rested since she'd brought the baby

home. Hadn't even had any time for the others, the way she had before.

Soon they might start crying, too, even though they had always been such good infants.

"What's wrong with you?" she demanded, looking malevolently toward the noise coming from the newest crib. "I've fed you, changed you, rocked you. You're supposed to be okay now. You're not behaving the way you're supposed to," she accused the infant.

Her words made no impression.

The noise continued.

It wasn't supposed to be this way. Everyone always maintained that infants cried for a reason. They were either hungry or wet or sometimes sick or in some sort of pain.

This one didn't want to eat. Everything she ate only backed up and came out again, or at least it did after a point.

The words echoed again in her brain.

It wasn't supposed to be this way.

She knew that. Hadn't she been a nurse in the maternity ward all those years, handling newborns? She *knew* how they behaved. If that stupid, stupid woman hadn't made such a fuss in the hospital, claiming that she was trying to take her baby from her, she would have *still* been working there, at the hospital. She was certain that she would be. And then maybe she could have had a chance to ask one of the other nurses—or even a doctor—what was wrong with her baby.

It was better to ask a nurse because nurses knew

more than doctors. Everyone knew that. Nurses worked the front lines while the doctors all clustered in the rear, issuing orders and occupying themselves with their golf game scores.

Useless people, she thought, frowning.

But now, for some reason, she had no access to anyone from the hospital. Nobody was returning her calls, no matter how many messages she left with the operator or on the answering machine when even the operator didn't pick up.

Why weren't they calling back?

She looked up, turning her head toward the new crib she'd purchased for this newest infant she'd brought into her life. Her head was splitting, and she could barely keep her eyes open.

The pain was getting worse, throbbing throughout her head.

"Why can't you be quiet like your sisters? They know when to stop crying. Why don't you?"

In response, the infant only wailed louder.

The woman took in a deep breath, willing herself to calm down.

The next moment she was on her feet, shuffling over to the source of all the discord within the nursery.

"Okay, okay, I'm sorry. I know you're not feeling well, and I shouldn't be raising my voice at you this way. It's just that it's been a long time since I heard so much crying, and I forgot just how much it got on my nerves. Your sisters are quiet. I thought you would be, too.

"I'll be more patient, I promise. But you have to try to stop crying, understand?" Her voice was shaky as she continued. "Otherwise, I don't know if I can be responsible for the way I react. I don't want to do anything bad to you, but you're peeling away all my nerves."

Her words had no effect on the infant she was addressing. If anything, the crying just grew steadily louder.

Hovering over the infant, leaning over the railing, she raised her hand, ready to strike, ready to do anything to make the noise finally stop.

At the last moment she backed away and grabbed the figure lying in the crib to her left. She clutched Adele against her ample chest. Just feeling her soft skin made her start to calm down.

"C'mon, Adele," she said to the tiny bundle in her arms. "Let's get out of here before I do something I can't undo."

Adele responded by trying to grasp her finger. The woman smiled as she exited the nursery. "You always know how to cheer me up, Adele. I'm sorry I brought Sara into our lives. She's keeping you up, isn't she?"

Adele just continued holding on to her finger.

If Andrew Cavanaugh looked surprised to see the young man standing at his front door, he gave no indication. Instead he greeted Shane the way he did all the members of his family: with warmth and cheer.

"C'mon in. It looks like it's about to pour any minute," he proclaimed. "The sky looks positively angry." Andrew glanced at the ominous streaks of dark gray and navy one last time before he closed the door. And then he asked the question he was most known for. "Hungry?"

Shane laughed. Incredible. His father had been right on the money. He'd thought that it was a joke. Until now, of course. "He told me you'd say that."

"You're going to have to be a little more specific than that, Shane," Andrew told him. "We've got a lot of 'hes' in the family."

Shane looked at him in surprise. "You know who I am?"

"Why wouldn't I?" Andrew asked, mildly amused that the young man would think that he didn't.

"Like you said, there are a lot of 'hes' in the family," Shane pointed out. On top of that, most of the men had the same dark hair, the same light green eyes. That made differentiation difficult.

"Doesn't mean I can't tell one from the other," Andrew laughed. "My eyesight's not failing, and neither is my mind. I'm not that old, boy."

"Didn't mean to imply that you were, sir." That wasn't exactly the way one went about setting the stage to ask for a favor, and he did want a favor. More than he first realized, now that he was actually about to ask. "And it was my dad who said that the first thing you'd do once you opened the door was to ask me if I wanted something to eat."

Andrew led the way into the kitchen out of habit. The kitchen was the place that he most frequently conducted any sort of business, now that he was no longer the chief of police.

He wasn't alone, Shane realized. The most senior member of the family, Shamus Cavanaugh, was there, as well, having coffee and a pastry that Shane assumed was homemade.

The family patriarch nodded at Shane as he came in behind Andrew.

"Do you?" Andrew asked, turning around to face him. "Want something to eat?" he repeated when Shane looked at him with a trace of confusion.

The confusion vanished as Shane shook his head. The last thing he was thinking about was eating. Hunger had no place here. "No, sir, I'm good."

Shamus was openly studying him as Shane came to the table.

"Which one are you?" he asked. "I'm not like him," he explained, nodding at his oldest son. "I haven't learned to keep all the faces straight yet. You were all a lot younger when I left for that miserable retirement hellhole in Florida."

"It wasn't a hellhole, Dad," Andrew said patiently. It had been his father's idea to retire to Florida in the first place, but he and Brian had checked the place out before their father had initially moved there. The reports from relatives of residents had been glowing. "It just wasn't exciting enough for the likes of you."

Shamus laughed dryly. "Now there's an understatement. Bunch of old people sitting around, listening to their bones creak. Life's too short to waste time like that," the older man complained. He looked accusingly at Andrew as he nodded toward Shane. "I still don't know which one this is."

Shane leaned over, offering his hand to the older man. He was surprised at how firm the handshake was. Older or not, the man's grip was still strong. "I'm Shane, sir."

Bushy eyebrows drew together in a single wavy, puzzled line. He looked at Andrew again. "Which one does he belong to?"

"He's one of Sean's sons, Dad," Andrew told him patiently, pouring a large mug of exceptionally strong coffee.

"Sean. The new guy," Shamus said, more for his own benefit than for anyone else's.

"Not exactly the new guy," Andrew countered. "But yes, for argument's sake, he's the new guy. Here," he said to Shane, pushing the steaming mug into his hand. Taking his nephew's free hand, he deliberately placed it around the mug, as well. "You're going to need this," Andrew hinted, slanting a telltale glance toward his father.

"Don't go filling his head with nonsense," Shamus warned, knowing exactly what his son was saying to the newcomer. Turning toward his grandson, Shamus told him, "He's just bent out of shape because he can't keep up with me."

"Don't mind him," Andrew advised Shane as he topped off his own mug of coffee. "He loves an audience. Now then, what is it that I can do for you?" he asked his nephew. "You definitely didn't come over to listen to the old man rant."

"Speak for yourself!" Shamus grumbled, raising his voice.

Andrew smiled. He'd gotten good at tuning his father out since the man had returned from Florida. It was a handy skill, given that they were now both engaged in trying to track down his father's long-lost brother. His father and uncle had lost track of one another more than half a century ago, when their parents had gone through an acrimonious split, each taking a son with them.

"So, what brings you here on such an inclement day?" Andrew asked.

Shane tested the waters slowly. "Dad said that you like to throw parties."

"Like to?" Shamus echoed, a dry laugh escaping, sounding almost like a cackle. "Does the Mona Lisa look like she's fighting trapped gas?"

"Eloquent as always, Dad," Andrew commented with a shake of his head. "But in his own unique way, what your grandfather just said was right. There *is* nothing I like better than throwing a party for the people whom I hold dear." Andrew got comfortable on the counter stool. "What did you have in mind?"

Shane figured he needed to clear something up first. "Well, this isn't exactly for someone you know."

Andrew inclined his head. He was not a stickler about things. "Is it for someone *you* know?"

"Yes, sir, it is." Not only that, but it was for someone he was hoping that he would get to know a whole lot better, he admitted to himself.

"Same thing," Andrew assured him. "Any particular theme or reason for the party?" he asked then, eyeing his nephew a bit more closely. "You're not looking to throw an engagement party for yourself and a lucky young lady, are you, Shane?"

The question threw Shane for a second, and all he could do was stare at his newly found uncle. "What? Um, no, it's not like that," he told the former chief, recovering. "That is, I mean, that's not the kind of party I was looking to have."

There was a strange, rather knowing smile curving his uncle's lips before Andrew gestured for him to lean forward. When he complied, Andrew told him, "Maybe you should start at the beginning. I'll try not to interrupt," Andrew promised him with an encouraging wink.

Shamus laughed, clearly entertained by this halting exchange. "Good luck with that," he said to Shane by way of an aside.

Andrew looked at the older man. "That goes for you, too, Dad. You interrupt and make more noise than an oncoming train."

"The hell I do. I'm quieter than a church mouse,"

Shamus responded, pretending to focus on the contents of his own coffee mug. The sly glance he directed at Shane gave him away.

Shane smiled to himself just before he got started. Unknown to the other two men, this exchange just served to reinforce the thought that this was exactly what his temporary partner needed to be exposed to.

Getting comfortable, Shane began at the beginning, just as Andrew had told him to.

Ashley looked at the man it seemed that fate had thrown her together with. They had methodically been going down the list of the baby boutique clients who had favored dealing with Monica while continuing to try to find other leads. Following the ones that had come up, they were making no headway exploring either path.

More than a week had gone by. A week where the only thing she'd discovered was that she was finding herself increasingly more attracted to the partner she was working with. Moreover, supposedly intent on solving the murder and finding the missing infant, Ashley found herself silently dreading it at the same time because then she would be going back to her position in Animal Control. And while she loved working with animals, and had an actual gift for it according to a couple of the other officers who worked with her, it meant that her reason for working with Shane would be gone.

Until she had begun, she had thought she would

be content working in this somewhat isolated world she inhabited. But now she looked forward to going in to work for another reason: dhe would be working with Shane.

This had to stop. She couldn't lose sight of the fact that she was an Animal Control officer, not a probationary detective-in-training.

Maybe someday, but not now.

She wasn't one who allowed fantasies to govern her life. She was a realist.

To get herself back in gear, she'd come in today, a Saturday, determined to make some sort of headway in the case that was threatening to go cold on them if they didn't crack it soon. She'd heard more than once that the more time that went by, the less likely it was that a kidnapped child would be found alive.

At this point, Ashley admitted to herself that for whatever psychological reason, she identified with the abducted infant.

Granted, no one had slashed her out of her mother's womb, but she had still found herself motherless, as well as fatherless, at an age where she could not recall having any family whatsoever. As far as she was concerned, it went without saying that the person who had kidnapped the infant and killed her mother was *not* someone who should be left to raise a child. It was a person who thought nothing of killing to get what he or she—and she was leaning toward she—wanted.

"I came in today to see if I could get anywhere

on the case," she told him in response to his question about what she was doing here on a Saturday.

She couldn't begin to guess why he'd been looking for her the way he'd claimed he was when he walked into the office, an exasperated expression on his face.

Oh, she knew why she *wanted* him to be looking for her, but she was intelligent enough to know that she would be dealing in fantasy, not reality, when it came to that.

She realized she was holding her breath, waiting for him to say something.

Shane forced himself to look calm. After getting Andrew to throw together a party, he would have been utterly embarrassed if he couldn't produce the person who the party was for. But she hadn't picked up when he called her cell, and when he'd gone by her house, she hadn't been there. Coming to the office had been his final attempt to find her. If she hadn't been here, he wouldn't have known where to look.

The tension within him began to abate. "That's really commendable, but you might get further if you stopped for a while and recharged your batteries."

"My batteries are just fine," she informed him. "And if you're worried about having to stay here with me, don't be. You can go back to your Saturday. I'm a big girl, I don't need a babysitter. I promise not to steal the silverware," she quipped. "Or plastic ware, as the case may be," she amended, thinking of what was available in the break room.

Rather than retreat, the way she thought Shane would, he moved around to the back of her chair and drew it—and her—away from the desk. Startled, she cried, "What are you doing?"

"Trying to get you to take a break," he told her. "Humor me."

"Is that part of the job description, humoring you?" she asked, not knowing whether she was amused, intrigued or just plain annoyed. There was something about this man that threw her whole world off kilter, set it on its ear and just got to her the way no one else ever had.

"It is today," he informed her cheerfully. "Weekends are for recharging and for getting different perspectives on things," he told her.

"What kind of different perspectives?" She almost yelped as she was all but deposited on the floor when Shane tilted her chair forward. She grabbed the armrests just as she started to slide forward.

He loosened her grip on the armrests, forcing her to plant her feet firmly on the floor. It was either that, or have her butt meet said floor. "Come with me and you'll see."

Left with no other choice, Ashley grabbed her bag. Less than a second later, Shane was steering her toward the doorway.

"Does insanity run in your family?" she demanded as she was being hustled out.

"Lots of things run in my family," he informed her calmly.

"Terrific," she muttered.

But he heard her and spared her a glance just before they headed out.

"Yeah," he told her. "Actually, it is."

"And just what's that supposed to mean?"

He made no effort to enlighten her. Instead all he would tell her was, "You'll see."

A weary sigh slipped out. "That's what I'm afraid of."

"Now you know that's not true," Shane contradicted. "You're not afraid of anything."

Despite the fact that she didn't try to dispute what he'd just said, Ashley definitely *was* afraid of something.

She was afraid of what she was beginning to feel for him.

Chapter 15

"Exactly where are we going?" Ashley asked, feeling herself growing restless and antsy in the passenger seat of his car.

Shane had talked her into leaving her car parked at the police station and going with him in the sedan rather than following him in her own small, close-to-ancient white Corolla. She had a feeling he'd insisted on taking her because he was afraid that she'd just make a U-turn somewhere along the line and head back to the precinct. This way he could control her.

She really didn't care for the thought. She'd been in control of her life ever since she'd turned eighteen, and she liked the fact that she didn't answer to anyone if she didn't choose to.

Part of being in control was knowing where you were going, and she didn't.

She glanced through the window. They appeared to be traveling through a residential area. Maybe Shane had changed his mind and decided she was right. They should work through the weekend, continuing to question more of the victim's legion of customers. So far, they hadn't had any luck, but there was always the hope that they might.

She'd never been an optimist by nature, but there was this small kernel within her, a tiny grain of hope that flowered on occasion. Sometimes it even mystified her that it did, but there was no denying its existence.

But if Shane *was* planning on doing more interviews, why wasn't he telling her as much? What was with this big mysterious act?

Shane spared her a glance. "You'll find out," he promised with a smile.

The smile was making her crazy. "You said that fifteen minutes ago."

"And I still mean it," he told her mildly. "Nothing's changed except that fifteen minutes have gone by," he pointed out cheerfully. "If you're going to be a detective, Ashley, you're going to have to learn how to be patient."

"And if you want to go on breathing," she informed him tersely, "you'll stop playing games and answer my question."

"I did answer your question," he pointed out, completely unfazed by her tone. "I just didn't give you the answer you were looking for."

She frowned. Now he was just bandying words about. "You sound a hell of a lot more like a lawyer than a detective."

"We've got a lawyer in the family," he told her, thinking of the chief of detectives' daughter, Janelle. "As well as a couple of judges." Those had married into the family. "Maybe it rubs off."

"Look, Cavanaugh," she began, a warning throbbing in her voice.

"Hey, we're here," he announced. Pulling up at the first curb space he found, Shane glanced in her direction and said, "Maybe you'd better call me by my first name. You say Cavanaugh around here, and you're bound to get a chorus of responses. That'll set you back by a while, I suspect."

Ashley looked around. He'd turned down a residential block. Considering the number of cars parked up and down both sides of the street, she was amazed that it was so silent in the area. Either the people who belonged to the cars had all been struck dumb, or this was the scene of some sort of macabre mass alien abduction. She wasn't sure exactly which explanation she was rooting for.

"Where's 'here'?" she asked pointedly, her eyes pinning him to his seat.

Or so she thought.

Shane was out of the vehicle and gesturing toward a house halfway down the tree-lined block.

"Here," he told her with a maddening emphasis that meant nothing to her.

Taking her arm, Shane began to usher her along the street and toward the house.

"And what is it we're doing 'here'?" She wanted to know. "And I swear, if you say 'you'll see' to me one more time, I'm not going to be responsible for what I do to you."

Their eyes met and held for a moment, and she could have sworn she both heard and felt a crackle of electricity so strong that for a moment she couldn't speak. She did her best to press her lips together into a frown.

"Stop," he teased. "You're getting me all hot with anticipation."

Now there was fire in her eyes as she all but shouted his name. "Cavanaugh!"

He stopped walking and raised his right index finger as if to caution her. "What did I tell you?" he asked as if he was speaking to a five-year-old. "What's my name?"

Her teeth were clenched as she tried to hold her temper in check. Why was it that this man could make her so angry so quickly? She prided herself on her even approach to things, her ability to mask her reaction. Around Shane, it seemed like it all went out the window.

"Mud as far as I'm concerned, if I don't get a few straight answers out of you soon," she told him.

He resumed walking with her again, and in a

minute they were on the doorstep of a large, rambling two-story house that seemed to literally exude warmth just by its very presence.

"Straight answers coming up," Shane promised as he rapped on the front door.

The door was opened by a tall, well-built man in his late fifties, possibly early sixties. It occurred to her that he carried his age well. It also occurred to her that he had to be a Cavanaugh. He looked like one of them. The man was wearing casual clothing and a wide grin, the latter being the very first thing anyone ever noticed about Andrew Cavanaugh.

"The door's open. You don't have to knock," Andrew told Shane, then added, "You made it." The former chief sounded very pleased. "And this has to be the birthday celebrant," he said, turning to look at her. He clasped her hand between his. Hers all but disappeared. "Pleased to meet you, Ashley. I'm Andrew Cavanaugh."

She would have been lost in awe of meeting the man if the first words he'd said to her hadn't left her completely bewildered.

"Birthday celebrant?" She threw Shane a perplexed took. "I think there's been some kind of a mistake. It's not my birthday."

"Oh? Are you sure?" he challenged. "Then when is your birthday?" Andrew asked, the voice of utter studied innocence.

"I don't know."

Ashley hated the way that sounded, hated admitting that she didn't know. It branded her as a person without a home, without a family to tell her the necessary things she ought to know. It made her feel like a rootless, homeless drifter.

"Well, if you don't know," Andrew began, "then how do you know it's *not* today? It might be, right? There is that possibility."

He had a point, she supposed. Still, she'd gone all these years without one—using July first, the day she'd been found near the burning vehicle, as the date she'd filled out on applications under date of birth, backdating the year by four because the first pediatrician that had checked her out had judged that she was in her fourth year.

But it wasn't her birthday any more than any other date was.

"Yes, but—" she began to protest. She got no further with Andrew than she had with Shane. Apparently none of the Cavanaughs took no for an answer—or brooked any sort of resistance.

Andrew tucked his arm through hers and brought her into the foyer.

"I was talking to Shane here about how he liked working in Homicide, and he started telling me about the partner he was temporarily paired with. When he mentioned that you'd never had a birthday party, well, I just couldn't let something like that slide."

He looked at her, and she could have sworn the very room seemed to light up. The man had probably charmed all his prisoners into handcuffs back in the day, she thought.

"So, for at least the spate of this party, today is your birthday and this is your birthday party." Andrew leaned over and whispered into her ear, "Everyone should have at least one birthday party they remember. Humor an old man," he added with a wink as he straightened again.

Her mouth had gone dry because it felt as if all the moisture she had available had gathered into tears and were threatening to fall now.

"All right," she managed to choke out in a whisper, agreeing to play along.

Andrew laughed, giving her a quick, one-armed warm hug.

"Atta girl." He turned toward Shane. "I'll leave the introductions to you. I've got a main course in the oven that requires my attention." He surrounded her hand with both of his for a moment and said just before he retreated, "Enjoy yourself. I'll catch up with you as soon as I'm able."

She turned toward Shane. "This was your idea, wasn't it?" It didn't come out like an accusation exactly, but it was obvious that she had an opinion on what the answer was.

"I haven't the vaguest idea what you're talking about," he answered innocently.

He eyed Ashley, wondering if she was going to be angry and accuse him of overstepping his boundaries or something along those lines. Instead, she surprised him by raising herself up on her toes and brushing a very soft, very light kiss along his cheek.

"Thank you," she whispered.

Her reaction left him utterly speechless for a moment. Then, collecting himself, he followed his uncle's advice and began to introduce her to the veritable legions of people who were otherwise known as Cavanaughs and Cavanaugh relatives.

The introductions took a long time.

At certain times during the hours that followed, and throughout the stand-up lunch, Ashley found herself making eye contact with one member of the gathering or another. For a brief moment, there would be a sympathetic look in their eyes, as if they thought they knew exactly what she was experiencing. But although they were undoubtedly well intentioned, she was convinced that they *didn't* know.

They couldn't possibly.

She'd been so utterly on her own right from the beginning, from the time she had her first vague memory. There'd been no mother, no father, no grandparent to turn to or to remember.

This, she couldn't help thinking, looking around at the various people on the premises, was something unique, something very special. What they had was something she had never had, and thus, they couldn't understand what she was feeling right at this second.

Envy and wistfulness.

"They're a great bunch of people," a redheaded

woman said as she came up behind her. "Until I met them, I thought people like this existed only in movies and books of fiction written for young teens." There was a smile on the woman's lips that softly whispered of genuine affection when she spoke of the people in the room. "They take you in, no questions asked, no judgments made. They just accept you, warts and all." She laughed softly to herself. "After having a grandmother who tried to sell me not once but twice—at least, twice that I recall—for drug money, something like the affection these people have for one another—and for you when they take you in—is really something very special."

Ashley stared at the young woman. More than the words, she absorbed the sentiment that the woman was conveying.

The woman's green eyes sparkled as she smiled. Putting out her hand, she said, "Hi, we haven't officially met yet. I'm Julianne White Bear Cavanaugh, the chief of D's daughter-in-law and Frank's wife," she added to help Ashley position her in the family dynamics.

"Ashley St. James," Ashley said mechanically, although she was rather certain that the woman already knew that. She tried to recall which Cavanaugh was "Frank" and whose son he was. These people should come with name tags. "White Bear, isn't that—?"

"Navajo, yes." Julianne nodded.

Ashley's eyes immediately went up to Julianne's flame-red hair. "But you have—"

"Red hair," Julianne completed for her. "Yes, I know. Long story." One that involved a kindhearted Native American police officer who rescued her from a life of hell. "I'll tell it to you one day," she promised. "Uh-oh, I think the chief's ready."

"Ready? Ready for what?" Ashley asked, confused.

She turned around to see what Julianne was looking at. She realized that the other woman made it sound as if she expected to see her again. Why would she think that? This was all temporary. She was temporarily Shane's partner and temporarily stepping inside his world, a world he could enjoy anytime he wanted. But she could only visit by invitation, and once they weren't working together, she was certain that the invitation would be rescinded. After all, why wouldn't it be?

Still, she couldn't help thinking that it was a really wonderful world.

"You'll see."

Surprised, she nearly jumped. The voice came from behind her. She swung around and saw that Shane was standing there, rejoining her after having stepped away for a few minutes.

Grinning, he repeated the line that earlier had had her threatening him with bodily harm. But before she could say anything or ask him just what he meant by the phrase this time, he deliberately turned her head with his hands, making her look forward again.

When she did, she saw that Andrew, flanked by his wife and a man she'd been introduced to earlier as Shane's grandfather, Shamus, was wheeling in a very long rectangular cake, decorated with pink and blue flowers, on a serving cart. There was writing on it that she couldn't see, and one very large candle in the middle that she *could* see.

Most likely, low-flying planes could see it, too.

"To commemorate your birthday as well as your first year among us," Andrew announced, bringing the cart with its precious cargo right up to her. Stopping, he looked around at his family, who needed no invitation to move closer. "Brace yourself," he warned her. "They're a great bunch of people, but harmonizing is *not* something they do well."

As if to prove him right, the people who filled the living room and surrounding areas all began to sing "Happy Birthday." At best, it could be described as a cacophony of words—and she had never heard anything lovelier in her life.

"Well, it's a guarantee that no one will ever approach this bunch with a recording contract," Andrew said as the song faded away. He turned to Ashley and coaxed, "Okay, Ashley, make a wish and blow out the candle."

Instead of doing as he urged, Ashley, overcome, suddenly turned away and hurried from the room.

Shane started to go after her, but Andrew held up his hand to stop him. "Let me," he told his nephew.

Frustrated, Shane remained where he was.

Andrew found her on the patio, an inclement sky threatening to rain on her at any moment.

"Ashley?" he said softly as he approached. "Are you all right?"

Her back to him, she raised her hand as if silently asking him to stay back. She didn't want him to see her crying. Not after he'd gone to all this trouble.

Andrew stood behind her. He talked to her back. "I know we're a little overwhelming at first," he admitted. "But we do grow on you if you give us a chance."

She couldn't allow him to take the blame for her fleeing the way she was. Turning around, wiping away the tears on her cheeks with the backs of her hands, she said, "Nobody has *ever* been this kind to me. *Nobody.* I don't know how to express my thanks. I've…I've never met people like you before."

"You can start by coming back and blowing out your candle," he told her. "The rest will work itself out. Right now, I'm sure Shane thinks you hate him."

"Oh God, no. I—" She stopped herself before she could make a fatal admission. Instead she said, "He's been very patient with me, putting up with a lot. I could never hate him."

"Then come back," Andrew coaxed, putting his hand out to her.

After a moment she took it hesitantly and went back with Andrew to the living room.

Conversation stopped the moment she walked in.

"She's agreed to give us another try. This time, I

promised we wouldn't overwhelm her. Don't make me out to be a liar," he told his family, taking them all in with one sweeping glance. "Ashley, I believe you have a wish to make." He gestured toward the cake.

She clenched her fists at her sides, doing her best not to cry again as she made a wish. The next moment, casting a side glance in Shane's direction, she took a deep breath and blew out the candle.

The applause was almost deafening. The sound was immensely comforting to her.

Andrew's wife, Rose, held out a knife to her. "You have to cut the first piece, dear," she prompted.

Taking the knife, Ashley carefully placed the blade against the top of a corner of the cake. The knife slid through it as if it was slicing softened butter.

When she finished cutting the piece, she moved it onto a plate.

"You get the first piece," Rose told her.

But Ashley handed the plate to Andrew instead. "No, you do," she told him, "for doing all this for me. For being kind to a stranger."

"Oh, honey." Teri, Andrew's middle daughter, laughed. "Dad just loves finding *any* excuse to throw a party. You just made his day."

Ashley surrendered her knife to Rose. "And he made mine," she said in a voice that was hardly above a whisper.

Shane stepped in and turned his body toward her

in such a way that he managed to temporarily block anyone else from seeing her at the moment.

"Are you all right?" he asked, concerned. After all, she'd run out of the room crying. He didn't want her upset, he wanted her happy. "You were crying."

"Must be something in the air," she said with a sniff.

He was willing to let her hide behind an excuse—for now. "Must be," he agreed.

And then she raised her chin defiantly, once again seeking refuge in umbrage the way she usually did. Except that this time, it felt somewhat awkward and stilted. "You could have warned me, you know. Given me some sort of a hint."

She was still very much a mystery to him, but this much was clear. "If I had, would you have come?" It was, as far as he was concerned, a rhetorical question.

"No," she answered honestly. She would have been too self-conscious, too sure that she was on the receiving end of pity. It took being here in person to realize that none of this was done out of pity, but out of a sense of sharing and warmth—and a genuine desire to make her feel wanted and a part of something, for however briefly.

"And that's why I didn't tell you, or give you any kind of a hint," Shane concluded.

"Hey, you two, don't forget to get your pieces," Lila, Brian's wife, called over to them. Crossing to where they were standing, she handed a plate to Ashley, then gave the other to Shane. Both pieces were on the large side. "Why don't you take her into the dining room, Shane?" Lila coaxed. "I think you'll find a couple of empty chairs there. If not, just tell whoever *is* sitting there that I said to let you two sit down. The lady of honor shouldn't have to stand at her own birthday party," Lila said fondly as she smiled at Ashley.

Patting her arm, Lila shooed them both out of the room and toward the dining room.

Her brother-in-law, she was willing to bet, was going to have another wedding in his future to plan.

In the not-too-distant-future, Lila amended, going off to locate her own prince charming. Brian was far too busy these days, and she just didn't see enough of him. She intended to make up for it tonight.

Lila smiled to herself as she withdrew.

Chapter 16

"You have an incredibly nice family," Ashley said to Shane.

It was hours after she'd made her wish and blown out the candle. The sun had long since gone down. She was sitting in his sedan, being taken back to the precinct to collect her own vehicle and head for home. Farewells and invitations to come back for another visit amid instructions "not to be a stranger, now" were still echoing in her ears.

She realized that although she knew the evening was over and that spending time with most of his family like this was almost certainly just a one-shot deal, Ashley found that she simply couldn't help smiling.

Her birthday wish had involved the impossible.

She'd wished she could be part of this terrific family, even though she knew it wasn't about to happen. The whole day had been magical, and just for a little while, she had allowed herself to believe.

Shane became aware of her wide smile immediately. Each time he saw it, he could feel himself reacting to it, could feel his pulse quickening. He'd given up trying to safeguard himself and shut out his reaction.

It was what it was, and he was just going to enjoy it. He'd be a fool not to.

"Yeah, I do," he agreed. "Although when I first found out about the connection, I was a little leery about being included in the roll call when someone referred to the Cavanaughs. To me, they were more like a dynasty than a family, but then, I only knew about them from hearsay, not direct connection." He laughed to himself. "That became a thing of the past quickly enough when Uncle Andrew got wind of Dad and the rest of us."

As he spoke, Shane heard the ominous rumble of thunder. It was unusual for this time of year, he thought. But then, this had been an unusual September all around. He'd be the first to admit it.

It was starting to rain again. Just enough to be annoying. "Sure I can't take you straight home?" he asked her.

"We left my car at the precinct," she reminded him. "How am I supposed to get to it tomorrow?"

That was simple enough. "I can swing by and pick

you up tomorrow morning, take you to it," he volunteered. "No big deal."

But it was, as far as she was concerned. "You've done more than enough for me," she told him. Feeling a little self-conscious and utterly unfamiliar with being in the position to have to convey her gratitude to someone, she murmured, "And if I didn't say it before, thank you for today."

"You did," he answered. "But you can say it again." He grinned as he turned down the block toward the station. "I don't mind hearing it."

Ashley stared down at her hands. She could face an animal on the loose calmly, but getting personal with Shane made her nervous and fidgety inside. "I know it probably seems silly, feeling like this about a birthday party. I mean, I'm over the age of twelve. But it did feel very special, and I won't forget it."

"It's not silly," Shane contradicted with feeling. "Birthday parties are important at any age. Everyone likes being remembered." Seeing that Ashley needed more convincing, he said, "Hell, birthday parties are one of the highlights of the chief's life. He probably enjoyed throwing you a party as much as you enjoyed being on the receiving end. Possibly even more."

She sincerely doubted it. She also doubted that Shane could really understand just how much this had meant to her. She would never forget the thrill that went through her when she realized what was going on—or when everyone sang "Happy Birthday" to her.

No one ever had before.

Feeling somewhat uncomfortable with all these emotions flowing through her, Ashley was relieved to see the police station come into view.

"You're almost free," she told him. "That's my car up ahead."

"I don't consider myself imprisoned or held captive," he told her. "This, in case you don't know, is what partners do—they do favors for one another. So do friends," he added significantly.

As he pulled into the precinct's rear parking lot, he admitted to himself that he really didn't want to drop her off here. He wanted to take her home. Hers or his, it didn't matter, as long as the evening didn't end yet. After spending the entire day and most of the evening with her, he found that he wasn't ready to call it a night yet.

But that would be forcing his company on her, he thought, and he didn't want to ruin the day for her by having her think he was being pushy.

She offered him a quick smile of thanks, as well as acknowledgment over the term he'd just used to label them.

Friends.

Was that what they ultimately were? Or was it more? Was it actually partners?

Or—?

She stopped her imagination from running off

with her. There was absolutely no point in allowing it to fill her head with things that couldn't be.

"Okay, you can just pull up here," she told him.

When he did, leaving the engine running, she unbuckled her seatbelt and said a quick, "Thanks again," just as she was about to get out of the sedan. But just before she did, she leaned toward him for a second and lightly brushed her lips against his. The slight contact gave birth to a second pass, a little longer, a little slower.

She could feel her pulse all but leaping out of her neck and her wrists even as her breath backed up in her lungs.

Taken completely by surprise, Shane absorbed the sweet sensation created by the touch of her lips to his. For a moment he anchored her in place, his hand on her shoulder as he kissed her back.

Kissed her back with feeling.

The next moment he felt her pulling away, a partially wary look in her eyes. Shane had no way of knowing that it was herself, not him, that she was afraid of.

The door closed in her wake even as he upbraided himself for going too fast. If this had been any other girl, the pace he'd taken would have been far too slow, but in her case he had a feeling that he was dealing with shadows of the past, and he had to go slowly to convince her that there was nothing to be afraid of when she was with him.

For a second he thought of apologizing, but decided that might only compound the problem so he let it go. Besides, she was already in her vehicle.

As he began to back out of the spot he'd pulled into, Shane heard her engine whining.

Once, twice and then a third time; each time unable to catch. Pulling back up beside her, he rolled down his passenger window. "Trouble?" he asked.

She nodded, staring accusingly at the nonresponsive engine. "I've been having trouble starting it lately."

It was raining harder now, Shane noted. This was not the ideal time to begin tinkering with the engine, even if he knew his way around them—which he didn't. That was Tom's domain, not his.

"Looks like you might have to take me up on that offer I made earlier—taking you home and then bringing you back here tomorrow. The rain should pass by then, and I can have my brother take a look at the engine for you—unless you want me to go get him now," he offered.

Asking him to do that, to inconvenience not just himself but one of his brothers, was out of the question. It was almost midnight, and the rain was beginning to come down in earnest. She really had no option but to take him up on his offer to give her a ride.

"Okay, if you don't mind taking me home, I'd appreciate it."

"I offered to take you home in the first place, didn't I?" he reminded her.

Still, it was obvious she didn't feel comfortable being on the receiving end of a favor. "But you could just be offering, to be nice."

"I *am* nice," he told her glibly. "But that still doesn't change what I said." Leaning over, he opened the passenger door and pushed it open. "Hop in and let's get going," he urged.

Grabbing her purse, Ashley abandoned her unresponsive vehicle and quickly got into his.

With the slick streets devoid of traffic, they arrived at Ashley's house faster than he thought they would. He pulled up in her driveway and turned off the engine. "Before you ask," he told her, unbuckling his seatbelt, "I like seeing a lady to her door, if it's all right with you."

"It's fine with me," she told him, her voice soft.

Ashley could feel the tips of her fingers tingling. It was hard for her to speak up with her heart in her throat the way it was. Anticipation had suddenly filled her to the bursting point. Anticipation that perhaps he wasn't going to go home the moment he walked her to her house.

That maybe he'd stay awhile and they could talk…

Who was she kidding? It wasn't talking that she had on her mind.

It was something a great deal more primal.

And exciting.

Because it was still raining, once she was out of Shane's car, she made a dash for the front door and shelter. Once she reached it, she shook the raindrops out of her hair.

Turning toward him, she offered, "Would you like to come in for some tea or something?"

"Are your dogs going to jump all over us the second you unlock the door and walk in?" he asked, quietly watching the door, braced for any sign of activity. The idea of refusing her invitation never crossed his mind.

"Just to make sure you're not a burglar," she assured him. But the corners of her mouth betrayed her as they curved into a grin.

He played along. Or maybe she was serious, he thought. Either way, he stayed alert and braced—just in case. "And how are they going to determine that?" he asked her.

"They'll recognize your scent, and besides, they'll see that you're with me." She put her key in the lock, then looked over her shoulder at him. "Ready?"

"Sure, why not?" he said with a cavalier shrug.

As she pushed open the door, all three dogs ran up to check her out, then the man standing behind her.

"He's okay, guys," she told the dogs. Taking Shane's hand in hers, she announced, "He's a friend, remember?"

Though Shane was skeptical about how much the dogs—any dogs—understood, it almost seemed to him as if the dogs *did* understand her. Their excitement dialed back several notches when she took his hand.

Conversely, his went up at the same time.

"They're still watching me," he told her in an even voice.

"They just want to be sure they're right about you. There's nothing to worry about," Ashley assured him as she led him to the sofa.

"If I kissed you," he proposed, "would they take it as an assault on you?"

A flash flood of heat all but drenched her as anticipation returned—in spades. "I don't know," she replied, trying to speak above the sound of her pounding heart. "Why don't you try and see?"

"Always ready to do things in the name of science," he said, then drew her into his arms almost in slow motion. Rather than watch the reaction of the three canines in the room, he was watching her.

Ashley could feel her breath all but standing still in her lungs, waiting.

And then his mouth lowered to hers.

The reaction, the excitement, was instantaneous.

At that moment she realized—she *knew*—this was what she'd been unconsciously waiting for all day. She felt as if her whole body had just burst into flame.

After several breathless seconds of his lips passing over hers, taking that kiss to deeper and deeper depths, she felt Shane draw his lips away from hers.

She saw him looking toward the dogs.

"So far, so good," she murmured encouragingly.

"No one ever just runs one test to reach a conclusion. Let's put it to the test at least one more time," he suggested, his eyes teasing hers.

She didn't wait for him this time.

This time, she was the one who began the kiss.

As for what happened next, she would have been hard pressed to say who initiated that or was responsible for all the steps that followed.

All she knew was that her entire body felt as if it was celebrating. As if it had been waiting an eternity just for this shining moment. For the mind-boggling kisses, the long, possessive caresses along her body that only created a desire for more, turning her appetite into an almost insatiable entity she was having difficulty controlling.

Hell, she wasn't controlling it at all, she secretly admitted. Instead, it was controlling her.

Her appetite was what was causing her to feast on his lips, to revel in the very touch of his hands. On the feel of his hard body pressing against hers.

It felt as if every inch of her craved him, wanting that final, wild burst of fulfillment—wanting, at the same time, for this to go on forever.

Shane hadn't thought it was possible to feel like this.

Not again.

He'd made love to more than his share of women before he'd fallen for Kitty. And while he'd been with her, there was such happiness radiating within him, he'd found it difficult to believe that he could place one foot in front of the other. That he could go on functioning as a human being, as a police detective when all of his limbs had turned to molten lava. But he could, and he had. Because he continued worshipping her body as he primed her for the ultimate act of sharing, of communion.

After Kitty had left him, he'd been fairly certain that he'd never feel this way again. And yet, here he was, not just feeling that wild, intoxicating sense, but experiencing something even more intense.

The emotion swam through him, almost drowning him, and yet he couldn't put a name to it, couldn't, if his life depended on it, begin to adequately describe the sensations slamming through his body, flooding every available space.

Desire was growing at an incredible speed, filling every single empty, aching inch of him.

But even while this all but overwhelming sensation was taking possession of him, he was aware that they had an audience.

Three small pairs of brown eyes were watching every move they made, separately as well as in concert.

There was no telling how long the dogs would refrain from trying to get in on the "game," however peripherally.

"Where's your bedroom?" he asked, realizing as he spoke that he was very nearly close to breathless.

It took Ashley a second to process his question.

When she did, it was another moment before she could actually form an answer to give him. She was thinking in single words, not sentences.

And nothing was processing except for this wildly insatiable need.

"Upstairs," she told him hoarsely.

About to get up from the sofa, she found herself being picked up in his arms instead. The next moment, her head swimming, she felt Shane walking toward the stairs with her.

As he reached the staircase, he sealed his mouth to hers. And then he began to carry her up the steps, one by one, prolonging her anticipation, creating a haven for her in his arms.

Utterly lost in desire, it took Ashley a second to realize that they had reached the landing.

He was waiting for instructions.

"First door on the right," she said hoarsely before he could ask, her desire for the ultimate union all but blotting out her already shaky thought processes.

She both felt and heard the door closing despite the fact that Shane continued to hold her in his arms.

Then suddenly, there was the bed beneath her. And then he was above her, his eyes making love to her moments before his body lowered onto hers.

When had her clothes come off?

When had his?

For the life of her, she couldn't remember the actual act of stripping away his clothing, or taking off hers. Had he done that?

Had she?

Her breath caught in her throat, then began to echo her frantic heartbeat as she felt him caress her over and over again before entering.

Felt his startlingly gentle first thrust.

The movement grew in momentum, in power. As it escalated, so did her reaction. By the time they raced over the peak together, Ashley was as breathless as if she had run a marathon in double-time.

The exhilaration that shuddered through her was indescribable.

She cried out his name even as she wrapped her legs around his torso, sealing him to her for all eternity.

Or at the very least, a little longer.

Chapter 17

Doing her best to understand, Ashley still had no idea how she had gotten to this place of frightened contentment.

She had never felt so happy and so afraid before in her life. So stable and yet so unsteady. At the same time.

All in all, it felt as if she was a walking mass of contradictions, and every single one of those contradictions could trace back its origins to Shane.

He was responsible for all the positive feelings going on within her and, in a general sort of undefined way, all the negative vibrations she was experiencing, as well. Not directly, but definitely in the form of the anticipation that shimmered within her.

It was the kind of anticipation involved in waiting for a second shoe to drop.

Ashley didn't trust being happy.

She didn't want to give this feeling up, but she knew that she had to. It was inevitable. It was just a question of when. After all, what went up eventually came down, right? It didn't stay hovering in the sky forever. She was braced for coming down and yet desperately wanted to fight it, to keep it at bay for as long as humanly possible.

She sighed. Maybe she was just going crazy.

"You know," Shane said to her as he looked across his desk to hers the following Monday after her birthday party, "my partner used to talk all the time. About everything and anything. Drove me absolutely crazy, and I would have sold my soul for a little peace and quiet just once in a while. But you're so quiet, it's like you're not here at all."

In the middle of yet another fruitless search on the computer, Ashley raised her eyes to his. "You want me to say something?"

"An occasional grunt will do if you can't think of anything," he told her. And then he looked around to see if anyone was within earshot. The squad room was relatively empty for a Monday midmorning. He moved his chair in closer to his desk to be closer to hers. He managed to make an imprint of the desk into his waist. Lowering his voice, he asked with concern, "Are you all right?"

An entire day had passed since the impromptu

birthday party and the glorious night that followed. She had hardly said anything to him when he'd dropped her off at her car yesterday, and this morning it seemed like just more of the same. He'd found her working when he came in. She'd looked up, spared him a quiet greeting and gone back to doing whatever it was she was doing.

Had she ultimately decided to be upset over what had happened between them? If she did, he needed to know so that he could find a way to fix it, to make her understand that it hadn't been just a casual night of sex for him. It had meant something.

And he wanted it to mean something to her.

"Yes, I'm all right," she told him, then asked, "Why shouldn't I be?"

"Well..." He looked around again to assure himself they wouldn't be overheard, then went on to say in a barely audible voice, "after two people make love, they usually open up a little to each other, not shut down completely like a rusty trap. So I just wanted to know if you're all right with what happened— Or if you're upset," he tagged on, watching her carefully for any telltale clues that gave him an answer to his question.

Ashley drew in a breath, then released it softly as she shrugged. "I guess I'm just waiting for the crash."

He was doing his best to read between the lines, but found that right now, the lines had been deliberately redacted, leaving him completely in the dark.

"The crash?"

She nodded. "The crash." Judging by his expression, what she was saying was obviously no clearer to him now than the first time, so she elaborated. "The bubble to burst. Cinderella to wake up. Judy Holliday to sing, 'The Party's Over.' You know, that kind of thing."

She was telling him in her own unique way that pessimism was creeping in. Not that he could really blame her. He was a little leery himself, especially after what he'd been through with Kitty. But as long as it meant that he could go on hanging on to this exhilarating feeling, he was willing to give it his all.

"Bubbles don't always burst, nothing needs to crash, and what if Cinderella wasn't asleep? She can't wake up if she's not sleeping," he pointed out. "And who the hell is Judy Holliday?"

"A movie star from the fifties. The song's from a 1956 musical, *The Bells Are—*"

"Stop," he pleaded, holding up his hand. "Tell you what. Why don't you just enjoy what's happening, and with any luck, it'll continue?"

"I can't."

"Why?" He wanted to know.

There was a very good reason for her to distrust what seemed to be happening. "Well, for one thing, because I've never been happy before," she admitted.

Ashley's simple admission stunned him. "Never?" he asked.

She shook her head. "Never," she repeated. "The best I've ever been is not unhappy."

Life, he thought, had so much to make up for to her. And he fully intended to lead the way—if she'd only let him. But right now, she needed to stop over-thinking everything. Otherwise, what was between them might not have a chance to grow. She'd wind up stifling it.

"Tell you what. Let's concentrate on the case and let the other thing take care of itself. It might surprise you," he quipped.

And it might not, she couldn't help thinking.

But in any event, Shane was right. The case came first. Everything else right now was just incidental. "I can't shake the feeling that the key to this whole thing is the baby."

He tended to agree, but he wanted to hear her thoughts on the matter. "Go on," he said encouragingly.

She'd been giving this a lot of thought. "Monica wasn't killed because someone wanted to get rid of her, she was killed because someone wanted her baby and she was in the way, so to speak. From what we know, it had to be someone with more than just passing knowledge of how to perform a C-section. I think we're looking for either a doctor or a nurse. Probably a nurse." She saw the skeptical look on his face. "You don't agree?"

"No, it's not that. But what if it's a guy doing it for his wife or girlfriend? Say she just lost a baby and is going off the deep end. He might have been trying to get her a substitute, saw Monica and felt like his prayers were answered."

Ashley nodded. She could see his take on it. "You've got a valid point. But it would still have to be someone Monica knew. That surveillance tape we have shows her letting the person into her apartment without any hesitation. If it was a stranger, she wouldn't have thrown open her door that way."

They agreed on that. It had to be someone Monica had recognized. "Well, since it doesn't look as if she had any kind of social life except for work, let's go back and talk to the boutique owner to see if maybe there's something we've missed," he suggested. He was getting restless, sitting here like this, just a few feet away from her and doing absolutely nothing about it. A little fresh air might do him good.

With no other options currently available, it sounded like going back to where the woman worked was their only available avenue of pursuit.

"Sure," she said, getting her purse out of the drawer. "Let's go."

When they arrived at the baby boutique some twenty minutes later, they were surprised to find the shop closed for business. Instead, the owner, the sales clerks and a number of people, some of whom they'd interviewed and recognized to be Monica's clients, were holding a small vigil. It was intended for Monica, to pay their final respects to the slain woman.

"What's going on?" Shane asked the owner as he and Ashley wove their way through more than a couple dozen people.

Abigail looked around at the crowded store and smiled sadly. "They all wanted to say goodbye to Monica. This was the next best thing," she told him. "By the way, I'm glad you're here," the woman said to them.

"How's that?" Shane asked, fully expecting to hear the woman say something about this proving that the police department had a heart.

Instead, Abigail Reynolds was glad they were there for a very practical reason. "The other day, when I gave you that list of Monica's customers, I somehow left one off," she confessed. "It's like the woman just fell through the cracks." As she spoke, she shook her head. "I don't know how I missed giving you this woman's name," she said. "She was Monica's exclusively. Monica was the only one in the store who could wait on her."

"Was that by request?" Ashley interjected.

Abigail accompanied her answer with a shrug. "That and the woman was so weird, she had a tendency to creep the other girls out. Only Monica was patient with her. She told me she felt sorry for the woman. According to what the woman told Monica, she'd gotten fired from her job and now was having trouble supporting herself and her children.

"You ask me, she couldn't have been having *that* much trouble," the woman commented. "The items she bought from us weren't cheap. But Monica has—*had*—" Abigail corrected herself "—a big heart. She even took the woman to lunch a couple of times. Oh God, I'm going to miss her."

"Would you happen to know what sort of job this woman was fired from?" Shane asked. He had a gut feeing about this. He didn't get them often, but when he did he was seldom wrong, and something told him they were on to something here.

"I think Monica said she was a nurse, or somebody who worked in the hospital." The owner shrugged, dismissing the other woman's story as fabrication. "Personally, I think she made it all up to get Monica's sympathy."

Shane's interest was totally piqued. "Do you have an address for this woman?"

The owner nodded. "Absolutely. We just delivered another crib to her house the week before Monica—" She couldn't get herself to complete the sentence. Instead she explained why she hadn't turned the woman's name over with the others when they were here the last time. "Her name and order form got mixed in with Sondra's clients," she said, referring to another saleswoman. "That's how I missed it last time," she admitted. "You wait right here. I'll get it for you."

"Think this could be it?" Ashley asked as the owner hurried off.

"God, but I hope so," he answered. For now, he said nothing about his gut feeling.

Abigail was back in a couple of minutes, holding out the page she'd just printed for them. Shane took it from her.

"I would have thought she'd be here," the owner said, referring to the client. "It's no secret that we were going to be holding a vigil for Monica. The girls sent out emails to all the clients." Her lips twisted in a sad smile. "It seems ironic that it's the same day that we were going to have Monica's baby shower." She shook her head, her eyes beginning to glisten. "She would have made such a wonderful mother," she said softly.

"I'm sure she would have," Shane replied with compassion.

"Detectives," Abigail began, addressing them both. "Is anyone claiming her body? The reason I ask is that I know she and her father didn't get along, and she'd said that he wanted nothing to do with her. So if he's washed his hands of her, I'd like to give her a decent burial—unless there's some rule against it."

"No rule," Shane told her. "I'll leave word for the coroner to release the body to you."

"Thank you," Abigail said sincerely.

"Don't mention it," he replied. Shane glanced at the address on the sheet she'd handed him before folding the paper and putting it into his pocket. "Let's go check this out," he said to Ashley. "I think it's about time we got lucky."

The address the boutique owner had given them took them to a residential area on the very outskirts of Aurora. Had it been located one block over, they would have officially found themselves in the neighboring town.

Unlike the other houses that populated the tree-lined block, the house where Monica's former customer lived was rundown in appearance. The garden was overgrown with weeds, and the building itself was sagging in places and in dire need of a new coat of paint all over. The facade was such that it fairly screamed of a termite infestation. The area just beneath the eaves was especially bad. It was obvious that the insects were still currently feasting in that section.

The person who owned the house was either unable to raise the funds to undertake repairs, or was completely oblivious to the condition of the house.

Shane had a feeling it was the latter.

"Looks like a house for a grade B horror movie," Ashley commented.

That impression was further reinforced by the appearance of a hole on the top step. The wood had obviously rotted through and given way when someone had made a misstep. Ashley took care to avoid it.

"At least the doorbell works," Shane observed when he pushed it and it chimed.

No one came to answer.

There was a car parked in the driveway, so he tried again. After a third attempt with no response, he tried the doorknob. To his surprise, Shane found that it was unlocked.

Glancing at Ashley, he asked, "You hear that? Sounds like someone yelling for help, doesn't it?" he said to her.

She knew what he was doing. They needed a plausible excuse to enter the premises. If the kidnapped infant was there, they were running out of time. Ashley played along.

"Sounds like that to me," she agreed.

Turning the doorknob, he opened the door at the same time that he carefully drew out his service revolver. If Monica's customer was their suspect, there was no point taking unnecessary chances. The person had already killed once that they knew of.

Ashley took out her own weapon. She'd only used it on the firing range, and the very feel of it in her hand under these circumstances felt strange. The weapon seemed oddly heavy to her.

They inched their way along through the eerily darkened hallway. Sunlight, so bright outside today, had not been invited into this place.

The entire house seemed as if it was built around menacing shadows.

There were a total of four rooms downstairs, each empty. By the time they reached the bottom of the staircase, Shane thought he heard noises coming from upstairs.

"Sounds like a woman singing," he whispered to Ashley.

"The store owner said that the woman had children, young ones who needed cribs," she recalled.

"Maybe she's singing to one of them, trying to get him or her to go to sleep."

Shane nodded. It seemed as good an explanation as any for now. He motioned for Ashley to follow behind him up the stairs. He didn't want to take a chance on her getting hurt.

He went up the stained, carpeted stairs slowly. Despite the carpet, he was afraid they might creak and he wanted to take no chances on alerting the woman they'd come to see—just in case.

Despite the care he was taking, one of the steps squeaked. He stopped, waited, and then proceeded when no called out to ask if anyone was there.

This felt like it was taking forever, Ashley thought. She could feel the muscles in her legs almost cramping up as they tightened in anticipation.

"This is going to be some letdown if we find out that it's nothing," she whispered.

Shane made no answer, but he was thinking the same thing.

He paused at the top of the landing, waiting for Ashley to catch up. Half a dozen scenarios played themselves out in his head before he went forward, prepared, he hoped, for anything.

Following the off-key singing, he made his way to what turned out to be the nursery.

The door was open, and when he looked in, he saw a matronly woman sitting in a rocking chair, swaying back and forth as she sang a tuneless refrain over and over again.

She was holding an infant in her arms.

An extremely thin, tiny human being who, by all appearances, had lost the strength to cry above a pathetic whimper.

Seeing the infant made him think of a rag doll.

As if sensing she wasn't alone, the woman in the rocking chair looked up.

Her first reaction wasn't surprise or fear. It was anger.

"What are you doing here?" the gray-haired woman demanded in a pseudo-whisper. "Go, leave. You'll wake the baby," she said accusingly.

"Ms. Wakefield," Shane began, addressing her respectfully, "we're with the Aurora police department, and we have some questions we'd like to ask you."

Her deep-set brown eyes narrowed even further as she glared at first one, then the other of her uninvited visitors. "No," she answered in a voice that was firm and no longer whispering.

The infant in her arms began to whimper, but still there was no cry. The sound was just barely audible. "You're upsetting my baby," Tessie accused angrily. "Now you get out of here before you make her start crying again."

One look at the infant and Ashley knew the baby needed medical attention. Somehow they had to separate it from the woman who was clutching the infant to her chest.

She was certain that this had to be the tiny human being who had been ripped out of her mother's womb by this heartless monster. If there was any further need for proof, it was obvious that the woman who was holding the baby was way too old to be the baby's mother.

Given this woman had so recklessly taken the infant without any regard for either life that had been so cruelly affected, Ashley knew she would have to be treated with kid gloves.

"What a beautiful baby you have," Ashley told the woman, moving forward in tiny, almost imperceptible increments. "I'd love to hold her," she said softly. Her eyes were on the woman's, doing her best to communicate with her, to form some sort of a bond. "Would you let me hold your baby? Just for a moment," she requested with all the sincerity she could manage. "You know, I had a baby just like yours once, but she died."

As she talked, she concentrated exclusively on the older woman. She didn't notice the look on Shane's face, or the way he was watching her.

"No one can understand what a huge heartache that is, losing an infant, investing a little being with all the love you have in you only to have that baby die, taking its promise with her."

With every word, she drew a little closer to the woman and the baby she was holding until she was almost within arm's length of them.

As if suddenly realizing what was happening, Tessie Wakefield rose to her feet, one arm tightening around the whimpering infant. Her expression belonged to a woman who was dangerously unhinged.

She looked capable of anything.

"Get back!" Tessie ordered, her eyes darting back and forth between the two people approaching her from opposite sides.

As she held the infant to her with one hand, the other dipped beneath the shawl that she had draped around her shoulders and partially around the infant.

"I said get out of here!" she repeated then, no longer mindful of the baby, screamed, "Now!"

To underscore her order, she pulled out a knife and held it to the baby's throat.

"Get out, or I'll kill her. I'll kill her before I let you take my baby from me!"

Chapter 18

"Don't do anything you'll regret, Tessie. I'm backing away," Ashley told the woman in as calm a voice as she could manage, given the circumstances. She'd raised her hands in a sign of surrender. "But all I wanted to do was hold her. You can't blame me for that. Your little girl's so pretty, she makes my heart ache."

Suddenly appearing to realize that she'd been focused almost exclusively on the approaching woman, Tessie looked around, still keeping the knife hovering menacingly by the infant's throat.

"Where is he? Where's the other one?"

"Right behind you," Shane said in a low, steely voice. While Ashley had distracted the woman by talking to her, he had managed to inch his way slowly until he was partially behind her.

Startled, Tessie swung around to get him in view. At the exact same moment—as if they had coordinated this and practiced it to perfection rather than spontaneously reacting in complete concert with one another—Ashley grabbed hold of the baby while Shane pulled back his doubled-up fist and punched the kidnapper right in her chin. Dazed from the suddenness of the blow, Tessie dropped the knife and crumpled to the floor, but not before somehow managing to drive the blade briefly into Ashley's shoulder.

Ashley was so intent on saving the infant, so utterly charged with adrenaline, she hadn't even realized the knife had slashed through her flesh until several minutes had passed.

Rolling the semiconscious kidnapper/killer over onto her stomach, Shane dropped to his knees to get the handcuffs on the woman while she was still groggy and couldn't offer much resistance.

Only after her wrists were secured did he say anything at all.

"We work well together," he told Ashley. And then, as he rose to his feet, he saw the blood. Her sleeve was wet with it. "Oh, damn."

"I don't think those two sentences are supposed to go together," Ashley quipped, her attention still utterly focused on the whimpering infant in her arms. "This has *got* to be the kidnapped baby. She's so tiny. I think we found her just in time." There was no doubt in her mind that even another day might have proved to be fatal for the baby.

As she tucked the baby more securely against her good shoulder, Ashley finally became aware of her surroundings. It took everything she had to keep her jaw from dropping. "Oh my God, Shane, look in the cribs."

Given her tone, it sounded as if they *had* stumbled onto a black market baby ring. Shane looked around the nursery. And saw that the other three cribs were indeed occupied. Taking a step closer, he reached out his hand to the occupant of the crib closest to him. The skin was amazingly soft to the touch.

His eyes widened. "Are those—?"

"Dolls," Ashley confirmed. "Those are called Almost Real Babies that some mail-order house has been coming out with for a few years now. I've seen ads for them on the internet," she told him.

Tessie struggled to get to her knees. "Don't touch them!" she shrieked. "Don't touch my babies! You can't touch my babies!"

"Okay," Ashley said, turning to look at Shane. She kept one hand protectively around the infant they'd just saved while holding the baby against her with the other. "I'm now officially creeped out."

"You're also officially bleeding," Shane told her.

The woman in front of him was still struggling to get up on her feet. The shock of what she could have done, stabbing Ashley as she fought her off, had his temper flaring. It took his last ounce of restraint to keep from dragging the woman to her feet. As it was, he yanked her up a little less than gently.

Meanwhile, Ashley was looking down at her arm. For the first time, she became conscious of the growing pain radiating along her arm.

"I guess I am," she answered, a little dazed. And then she looked at the baby she was holding. "But the important thing is that we got you back, isn't it, sweetheart?"

"Give me back my baby!" Tessie demanded, trying to break free.

Shane's hold on her tightened as he restrained the woman. "That's not your baby," he told her gruffly, then ordered, "Now shut up." Holding her in place, he pulled out his cell phone and called for an ambulance for both the baby and his partner. He wasn't about to put up with any trouble getting through and being heard.

As if sensing that the police detective had been pushed as far as he would go, the older woman became subdued. Within a moment she appeared to have retreated from reality altogether, rocking where she stood and mumbling to herself.

Ashley rode in with the infant in the ambulance. Her main concern was to get the baby checked out, but her arm was beginning to severely ache and she decided that getting bandaged up herself wouldn't hurt, either.

Shane had gone on to the precinct with their prisoner. The sooner the woman was behind bars, the sooner she would breathe easy, Ashley thought.

The trip from Tessie's house to the hospital was extremely short. Nevertheless, by the time the ambulance arrived at the E.R. entrance, Ashley found that she had bonded with the baby.

Even though she was bleeding, she insisted on being there with the infant while the doctors took care of her. The attending physician in the E.R. was far from pleased, but her response to him was that she wasn't interested in winning a popularity contest; she just wanted to be sure that the baby was going to be all right.

"Isn't there anyone in the police department who isn't so damn stubborn?" the E.R. physician demanded. It was obvious that he was familiar with the Cavanaughs, who were less than patient when they needed to be treated at the hospital. He beckoned over one of the nurses.

"Possibly, but they're on desk duty," Ashley answered.

"See what you can do about getting that wound of hers cleaned up. Last thing we want is Brian Cavanaugh getting on our case about letting one of his people bleed to death."

"Don't worry, I'm not one of his people," Ashley told the doctor as she was being ushered over to the side of the exam room.

"You're with the police department, aren't you?"

he retorted, never bothering to look up from the infant he was treating.

Ashley made no answer as she continued watching the doctor work over the infant she and Shane had rescued. But she smiled to herself. The feeling of being part of something and being taken care of was very new to her, and she liked it.

Ashley was checked out, sewn up and told to go home and rest by the resident who wound up taking care of her.

"And the baby?" she asked as she watched the infant being wheeled out in a glass bassinette. For lack of a name, they had written in hers on the base of the container.

Seeing it took her back.

The resident paused to write something on the chart that detailed what he'd done to her. "We're going to keep her here for a few days, run a couple more tests to make sure she's all right. Don't forget, she didn't exactly have a typical birth process. According to Dr. Riley's estimate," he said, referring to the E.R. physician, "the baby was a little shy of full term when she was taken from the womb."

"Would it be all right if I came and visited her?" Ashley asked. There were a great many more safeguards on the maternity floor these days, and she wanted to make sure she could gain access without causing a disruption in the routine.

The neonatal specialist who had been called in to

consult on Monica's infant heard the last part of her interaction with the resident. His gray eyes crinkled as he smiled at her. "I think that might be very good for her. Babies are never too young to make connections, and they respond to being touched and handled far more than was once believed."

He regarded the sling she had newly acquired. There was concern when he raised his eyes to hers. "I'm told that Aurora has the most invincible police personnel, but is there anyone to take you home?"

"I'm taking her home."

Startled, Ashley turned around to see Shane walking toward her. He must have just arrived, she realized. The last she'd seen of him, he was taking the deranged former nurse to the precinct to be booked.

"Then I leave her in your capable hands, Detective," the specialist said, withdrawing. He said one last thing to Ashley before going to attend to his next patient in the pediatric ward. "Remember, *rest.*"

Ashley's response was a spasmodic smile before turning toward Shane. "Why aren't you in booking?"

"I got my sister, Kari, to finish processing Miss Loony-Bin." He didn't add that his concern for her had him rushing back. But his eyes said as much as they swept over her. "So you're okay?"

"Just a scratch," she replied with a dismissive shrug.

"That 'scratch' was bleeding like a sieve back at the crazy woman's house," he pointed out in a no-

nonsense voice. "You do realize that you're not immortal."

She tossed her head. "Yes, I realize that and I'm fine now." Ashley didn't want to waste time talking about herself or how she felt. She was more curious about what he had learned about the woman who had kidnapped Monica's baby after killing Monica. "Did you find out anything about that awful woman?"

Very slowly, he began to guide Ashley toward the rear doors. He'd left his sedan in the E.R. parking lot. "There were all sorts of signs that she was crazier than a March Hare. It turns out that Tessie Wakefield was a nurse who was fired from the hospital where she worked because she tried to keep a baby from its mother."

"What did she do?" Ashley asked.

"She claimed that the woman was unworthy of being a mother. The woman started screaming. Luckily, another nurse rushed in to find out what was going on. She managed to placate the patient. The upshot of the whole incident was that no charges were pressed, but Tessie was fired."

Shane paused at the E.R. reception desk to sign her out, then slipped his hand to the small of her back and gently ushered her out the door.

"A nurse," Ashley repeated, shaking her head. "That would explain the attempt at a C-section," she said. It had been far from perfect, but it did indicate that whoever had done it knew their way around anatomy.

Shane paused. "You want to wait here while I get the car?"

"I'm not an invalid," she protested with feeling. "I can walk."

"Nobody said you couldn't," he countered. But just to play it safe, he tucked her hand through the crook of his arm. Only then did he begin to walk to where he had parked his vehicle. "What'd the doctor say about the baby?" he asked.

"We can walk faster than an arthritic snail," she prompted.

"Yes, we can," he agreed. But even so, he didn't pick up his pace.

Ashley gave up and turned her attention to his question. "The E.R. doctor said she appeared surprisingly well considering the enormous trauma she'd been through. They're going to keep her here a couple of days to make sure they haven't overlooked anything." She hesitated for a moment, then told him, "Instead of writing Baby Phillips on the outside of the bassinette, the nurse put my name on it."

"That's nice," he said without actually paying that much attention to what she'd said. He was, however, distracted by the expression on her face. Ashley was pressing her lips together.

"Something's on your mind." It wasn't a guess. Shane was beginning to pick up on all her signs. "What?" Reaching his sedan, he unlocked her side first and held the door open for her.

Feeling suddenly drained, Ashley sank down in

the seat and was secretly grateful when he pulled out the seatbelt for her and buckled her up. She suddenly had the energy of a flea.

"I don't want her to go through what I did," she told him. Because she knew she was throwing a disjointed fragment of a thought out of left field at Shane, she backtracked. "That baby has no one who wants her. It was clear her father doesn't, and her grandfather would sooner have her burned at the stake as the spawn of Satan than take her in."

Ashley had already made up her mind about what she was going to do, but since Shane was part of the baby's rescue, she felt he deserved to hear this from her. "I want to adopt her."

Shane was well aware that his temporary partner didn't march to the same drummer the rest of them did, but what she was proposing to do was surprising even for her.

"Whoa, that's a big step." He slid in behind the sedan's steering wheel. "Why don't you sleep on it?" he suggested. "See how you feel in the morning."

"The time of day isn't going to make a difference, or change my mind," Ashley insisted. "I *was* that little girl twenty-one years ago. I know what she's in for, and I can keep it from happening." She was determined to see this through, and she wanted him to understand why she felt so compelled to do this. "Single women adopt babies all the time."

"True, but that's not the only thing social services

and the judge look at. They look for a stable lifestyle, and you're in a dangerous profession," he pointed out.

She laughed shortly, recalling what he'd said to her the first time they'd met. "I'm a glorified dog catcher, remember?"

He pulled out of the lot and drove onto the main street leading away from the hospital. "You're never going to let me forget that, are you?"

"It was true," she told him. "And there's nothing dangerous about picking up roadkill."

He spared her a look as he stopped at the first intersection. "What about your dream of moving up in the department?"

A child's life was far more important than a career, Ashley couldn't help thinking. "There's been a slight change of plans," she told him glibly.

He hadn't wanted to point this out, but she gave him no choice. "There's also the fact that you don't have a family—there's no backup support system to help you in case you get sick or something else comes up."

The light turned green, and he put his foot back on the gas. He wanted to get her home as soon as possible. He wanted to discuss this major life event with her without being distracted by traffic or anything else.

But this wasn't going to wait another fifteen minutes. He needed to tell her *now.*

"You know, they'd be more inclined to let you

adopt a baby if you were married—or at least engaged to be married," he said matter-of-factly.

Ashley laughed shortly. There was no sense in going there. She had to deal with reality, with the hand she was dealt, not with some wistful pipe dreams. "I can't exactly advertise for a fiancé now, can I?"

"No, I wouldn't advise it," Shane agreed. "But that wasn't what I was saying."

What were you saying? Ashley couldn't help wondering. "What? You're telling me that you know where I can find a fiancé lying around somewhere?"

He squeaked through a light a second before it turned from a forgiving yellow to a forbidding red. "As a matter of fact, I do."

Why was he doing this to her? Did he think she'd find it funny? She was serious about adopting that little human being and, in an ideal world, he would be the man at her side.

But *nothing* had ever been ideal for her, and there was no reason for her to believe that it would start now. The man had utterly rocked her world the other night, but she was a big girl and she knew that people like her didn't get lucky like that very often.

"Yeah, right," she said mockingly. "Who?"

"Me," he told her simply.

Now that was downright cruel, she thought. Did he suspect how she felt about him? Was this his way of driving her away, by poking fun at her? "Very funny," she answered coolly.

"I wasn't trying to be funny." His voice was so serious, she stared at him, waiting for that shoe to fall, the laughter to begin. How far was he going to carry this joke?

What if it's not a joke? a little voice whispered in her head. *What if he's serious?*

The next moment, he said as much.

"I was trying to be serious. I *am* serious. You're the kind of woman I've been looking for, Ashley," he said. Then, because a man couldn't bare his soul to the woman he loved while driving, Shane pulled over to the first empty parking area he saw, turned off the engine and then turned in his seat to look at her. "A woman who can be a partner," he continued as if there'd been no pause at all, "who won't ask me to give up something I feel defines me as a person."

Her mouth was dry, and she could feel herself trembling inside. "You can't be serious," Ashley insisted. "You don't know me. You don't know anything about me."

"I know enough," he answered. And as far as he was concerned, he did. There was something about her that spoke to him, that reached him in the furthest recesses of his soul. "But if you feel you want to further enlighten me, go ahead."

There wasn't a single drop of moisture in her mouth. The words felt as if they were choking her as she pushed them out. "I had a baby."

He'd already gotten that impression by what she'd said to Tessie when she was attempting to calm her, but since she didn't actually mention one and there were no photographs of a child in her house, he had the feeling that this part of the story didn't have a happy outcome. He was waiting for her to say something in her own time. He'd never believed in pushing an issue.

"Go on," he coaxed quietly.

She stared straight ahead. "My baby was stillborn. The father had long since been out of the picture. It took me a while to get my head back together." She looked at Shane now, waiting for him to comment. When he didn't, she asked, "Well, aren't you going to say anything?"

He hadn't wanted to interrupt her or to say anything until she was finished. "I'm sorry."

She waited for more. There wasn't any. "That's all?" she asked incredulously.

"I wish I had been there for you," he added.

That wasn't what she meant. She thought there'd be accusations of secrecy, or that he would use it as an excuse to withdraw the emotional support she felt coming from him.

"You're not surprised I kept that from you?"

He shook his head. "It's not exactly something someone can fill in on a résumé," he answered. "Your past is your business. If you don't want to talk about it, I'm okay with that. It's your future that's my business, not your past. Now, getting back to my proposal," he said glibly. "I don't expect an answer from you right away, but the offer *is* on the table. I love you, and I'd like the chance to make up for the lousy hand that life dealt you prior to this."

She stared at him, wondering when she'd begun to hallucinate. But he was still there, waiting for her to say something. "You're serious."

He thought they'd resolved this already. Apparently not. "Why wouldn't I be?"

For a very simple reason. "Because good things don't happen to me."

"That was the old you," Shane said, dismissing that persona. "Good things do happen to the new you."

Ashley was still unconvinced. "I don't want your pity," she insisted.

"But I want yours."

Okay, now he wasn't making *any* sense. "What?"

"I want you to take pity on me," he said, spelling it out for her. "I don't think I could handle being rejected. I went through it once, and it took me a while to glue together what was left of my tattered self-esteem," he told her in all seriousness. "If you reject me, I'm not sure that I'll be able to recover."

Pausing for a moment, he went for broke.

"I had a feeling about you when I first met you."

She remembered every detail, every look that had passed across his face. "Yeah, you thought I was a pain in the butt."

"And I wasn't wrong, you are," he replied matter-of-factly. Then, before she could say anything in response, he told her, "But I also had a feeling that we belonged together. That the sum of us together is even greater—even *better*—than the parts."

He was serious. He was really serious. Oh, wow, she thought, too overwhelmed to speak for a moment. And then she did, proceeding cautiously.

"All right, we'll get engaged," she told him, not letting on just how hard her heart was pounding right at this moment. "And I'll give you six months to come to your senses."

"What happens after six months?" he asked, watching her expression.

She chose her words very, very carefully. "If you're still willing to tie yourself down to me after six months, then it's okay with me," she told him, trying her best not to sound breathless. "We'll get married."

"Is there a fast-forward button on this thing, by any chance?" he asked. "A way to turn six months into six minutes, something like that?" A trace of his impatience rose to the surface.

"I'm afraid that would defeat the purpose." *Of you coming to your senses,* Ashley concluded silently.

"Okay, then we'll do it your way. We'll be engaged for six months. They'll be six of the longest months of my life," he added. "But if that's what'll make you happy, I can stick it out." His expression remained serious as his eyes searched her face. "But I get to kiss you during those six months, right?"

Now it was getting decidedly hard for *her* to maintain a serious expression, as well, especially since the way Shane was looking at her was making her feel exceedingly warm, not to mention aroused.

The word almost stuck to her throat, but she finally managed to get it out. “Right.”

“Good.” He made no attempt to start the car again. “I sure hope you bought stock in ChapStick ’cause you’re going to be using a lot of it,” he told her just before he showed her why.

Five minutes later, as he stopped for a breather, she murmured, “Maybe we’ll make that three months.” She felt rather than heard him laugh.

“Sounds good to me,” he responded just before he kissed her again.

Shane fully intended to pare the months down to zero.

* * * * *

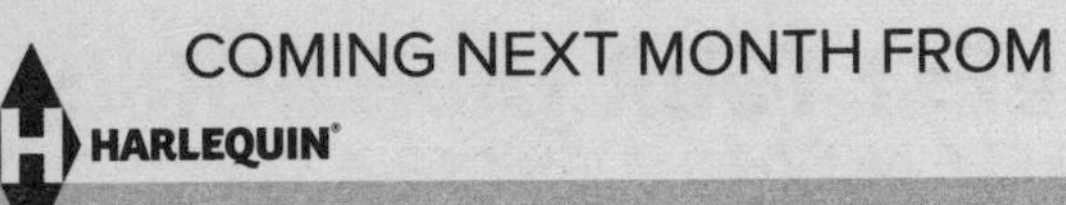

Available October 1, 2013

#1771 KILLER'S PREY

Conard County: The Next Generation
by Rachel Lee

After a brutal attack, Nora Loftis returns to Conard County and the arms of Sheriff Jake Madison. But her assailant escapes, and he's coming for her. Can Jake protect her and heal her soul?

#1772 THE COLTON BRIDE

The Coltons of Wyoming • by Carla Cassidy

Heiress Catherine Colton broke rancher Gray Stark's heart, but when danger surrounds her, he steps up. A marriage of protection will keep her safe, but he finds his heart at risk.

#1773 TEXAS SECRETS, LOVERS' LIES

by Karen Whiddon

With her best friend missing, Zoe risks her life to find her, but she can't do it without Brock McCauley, the man she left at the altar five years before—and never stopped loving.

#1774 THE LONDON DECEPTION

House of Steele • by Addison Fox

When a sexy archaeologist teams up with a mysterious thief to unearth a cache of jewels in Egypt, the competition turns deadly and the only person either can trust is each other.

SPECIAL EXCERPT FROM

HARLEQUIN®

ROMANTIC suspense

To unearth a cache of jewels in Egypt, a sexy archaeologist teams up with a mysterious thief from her past.

Read on for a sneak peek of

THE LONDON DECEPTION

by Addison Fox, available October 2013 from Harlequin® Romantic Suspense.

Rowan wasn't surprised when Finn followed her into the elevator, but she hadn't counted on his rising anger or the delicious sensation of having his large form towering over her in the small space.

"I can explain."

"I sure as hell hope so."

"Rowan. Listen—"

"No." She waved a hand, unwilling to listen to some smooth explanation or some sort of misguided apology. "Whatever words you think you can cajole me with you might as well save them." The elevator doors slid open on her floor and she stomped off.

She was angry.

And irrationally hurt, which was the only possible reason tears pricked the back of her eyes as she struggled with her electronic key.

"Here. Let me." Finn reached over her shoulder and took the slim card from her shaking fingers. The lock switched to green and snicked open.

She crossed into the elegant suite and dropped her purse on the small couch that sat by the far wall, dashing at the moisture in her eyes before he could see the tears.

"Rowan. We need to talk."

"You think?"

"Come on. Please."

She turned at his words. "What can you possibly say that will make any of this okay?"

"I couldn't tell you."

"You chose not to tell me. There's a difference."

He was alive.

The young man who she'd thought died saving her was alive and well and living a life of prosperity and success in London.

"Do you know how I've wondered about you? For twelve long years I've wondered if you died that night. I've lived with the pain of knowing I put you in danger and got you killed."

"I'm fine. I'm here."

"And you never even thought to tell me. To contact me or give me some hint that you were okay. That you'd lived."

"It's not that easy."

"Well, it sure as hell isn't hard."

HRSEXP0913